eyes of a sociopath

Eyes of a Sociopath
© 2012 by L. R. Sheridan

ISBN: 978-0-9882616-0-0
Library of Congress Control Number: 2012916523
Printed in the United States of America

eyes

OF a SOCiOPaTH

L. R. SHeRiDan

CONTENTS

DEDICATION

*For those who know what it's like to be
caught in the crosshairs of a sociopath
and others who have yet to be; changed forever by an
experience they will surely take to their graves...*

INTRODUCTION

"DO YOU REMEMBER ME? I WAS STANDING BY THE PORTER wearing my favorite blue dress with white sequins. You glanced at me from across the foyer. I rushed out to follow you, but I was too late and I saw you driving away. Luckily, I wrote down your license plate number. I called you a couple of times but you didn't answer. Was that your girlfriend? You don't need her anymore. I'm here now. She can't give you what I can."

Amanda is a sociopath. Impulsive, beautiful charming and unpredictable with a fashion sense that could shame a runway model. Reports from her doctors say she was born without a conscience and is unable to feel remorse, guilt, or love.

Prepare yourself for the unthinkable, because the story of Amanda's life will introduce you to a separate but parallel existence reserved for a chosen few. Her story is bound to confirm your gut feelings about certain people you have met. People who are not what they seem.

Open your mind to the fact that a sociopath can be a best friend, lover, family member, or the person living next door. Disturbing as it may be, it's a real possibility, and most likely, they blend in seamlessly and you would never know, until it's too late.

Amanda, like most other sociopaths has an exceptional intellect and likeability, a lethal combination. Not a serial killer, but a functional person who learned to mimic the behaviors of others the best she could, to fit in. She was able to equip herself with the characteristics of a kind, caring, and compassionate individual. A choice she made in an attempt to live her life as normally and productively as she could.

Still, in the world she created, there is an element of naïveté because of her inability to experience human connection. Many of her actions and behaviors are a result of her diagnosis, and play out in her daily life as devastation and destruction to unsuspecting people she comes in contact with. To Amanda, there are no rules, only lies and sexual manipulation; risky and dangerous behavior.

Like many sociopaths, at fourteen, Amanda recognized she was different. Her intellectual ability, combined with her talent for acting, pushed her to appear more loving and sincere than a real feeling person. To her credit, she mastered the ability to exhibit tears and emotions at will. Amanda strove to survive, and within that context you will understand that a sociopath acts and reacts based on information they are processing most of the time without our knowing. They operate steps ahead; therefore they can target anyone in any occupation, including family and friends, for reasons that seem cold to you and me, to bystanders and those who dare stand in their way. In their minds, it is a logical process.

Each day for Amanda is exhausting, a never-ending effort to hide the absence inside of her. An emptiness that leads to envy, frustration and a desire to destroy others who have what she cannot—true happiness.

"Once the stage has been set, it is controlled by me, and if you're my target, you will be helpless and unaware until it's too late for you to do anything to stop me. There is no warning and I always win," she said.

"I may choose to like you, love you, or destroy you—in some cases all three—with or without notice. Each time you move, speak, or walk, I am learning you. I can exploit your weaknesses and manipulate everyone you care about to distrust you…hate you. I have the ability to fool you and everyone else with compassion that will blow your mind. When you're no longer useful to me, my mind will have developed a strategy to ultimately lead to your downfall. When I'm done, you will be screaming for me to get out of your head; then, when I do, you will beg me to come back because you need me. I will test the limits of your human soul."

Highly intuitive, Amanda can read almost any person in an instant. She has also developed the ability to detect the scent of another human being as their body secretions give off unique and specific odors when experiencing certain emotions. This helps her sense fear, anger, and stress levels. "When I've targeted someone and they are not reacting to my liking, whether it is agonizing pain or an impending desire, I turn it up, just like turning up the flame on a stove," she said.

For Amanda, it's just an exercise, a process to win at all costs, designed to damage the human spirit.

"There are thousands of men and women out there just like me. We see you shop at your favorite boutique and watch while you play with your kids in the park. We stand in plain sight, yet we remain undetected. We fool you because you don't know that we are wearing a mask. It's easy because people like you see what you want to see. We study you and wait for the right moment when your guard is down. Then exploit you for our own benefit and you don't even know it."

"You are our prey and we are always hunting."

PROLOGUE

LIKE A FLEETING THOUGHT IN THE MIND, I BEGAN TO FEEL a hot steady breath on the nape of my neck. The hairs on my arms stood in anticipation, and I felt a strange and unexpected excitement, which I discounted as an invigoration, probably from the wine I had earlier. This was followed by the deep sweet smell of jasmine. As I turned, I suddenly found myself face to face with a woman seated next to me. Stunned by the close proximity of her face to mine, I was breathless. She was too beautiful for words. I sat unable to collect the courage to begin a brief introduction.

With the bluest, most piercing eyes I had ever encountered, she glanced down to observe my name. Hers said Amanda. The woman turned away, shifting her chair to watch her male companion as he walked to the stage.

The gala was held to recognize ten individuals (and their organizations) who had been selected to receive a coveted annual award for helping underprivileged kids in Northern California. The Empire Ballroom at the Sir Francis Drake Hotel on Union Square was the perfect setting for the glamorous donors and philanthropists present who were looking for a place to invest their money.

Although there were only sixty or so people in attendance,

everyone in the theater stood to applaud the beginning of the ceremony and to recognize this year's recipients. Throughout the evening, each would be given the opportunity to describe how their privately funded programs had helped low-income families.

Looking up toward the stage, I noticed the woman's male friend had taken a seat next to my wife. I felt compelled to speak to the woman to inquire which urban community her friend was being recognized for helping; but I refrained, deciding to wait until later when there was a break in the presentations.

Seated at a table for four, but with only two of us present, I glanced back at the woman next to me named Amanda. The warm amber lighting in the room revealed a slender, attractive woman with blonde hair that shone. The contours of her cheekbones were accented, dressed with a subtle flush. The red gown touching her pale skin drew my eyes to her full red lips. In the background, the gold leaf accents on ivory, and rich murals on the walls seemed to play off her exquisite coloring and style.

As I sat through the ceremony, I felt slightly impatient, reminded that the evening would likely be long and boring, as these things sometimes are; with introductions, thank yous, the usual sweaty handshakes, short speeches, hors d'oeures, let's get togethers, nice to see yous, and the ride home accompanied with a brief dissection. I had hoped at some point to sneak off to the bar for a few minutes to catch the Forty Niners halftime score.

After the introductions ended, I was surprised when the woman leaned to me and whispered, "Hi, handsome." I blushed and smiled, complimented and mesmerized by her introduction. "Hello, pardon me," I said. "My face gets red after I've had a glass or two of wine." She responded with a laugh and a light touch to my forearm. For a moment, I became fixated on her beautiful smile; I also laughed, trying to hide my giddiness as if on a first date.

I was reminded of my wonderful relationship with my wife and felt a bit embarrassed at our flirtatious exchange, so I quietly asked what her involvement was with children's programs. She said it was her friend's special night, but she typically didn't attend these types of ceremonies.

"I've been busy with several projects of my own and my attendance was rather abrupt," she said.

She was very polite, and favored a strong upper-class style and grace—a confident, well-rounded woman. Since I too was here at the request of someone else, we shared an immediate connection.

As the ceremony continued, we remained the only two seated at our elegant table; I imagined we probably looked like a couple together: me, the slightly older man who most would assume had money in order to attract such a ravishing younger wife. Thankfully, the waitstaff came around with more libations, causing a much-needed distraction. Just enough to give me time to see my wife sitting through another round of speeches in what probably seemed endless.

I tried not to stare at this woman in her tight, sleek red gown seated next to me, but I was stimulated by her mysterious nature. My curiosity was unusually heightened and it began to create a hunger in me to learn more. I began to guess at what type of occupation she might have. My mind pictured her as a stockbroker on Wall Street, or maybe a doctor of neurology, or perhaps the daughter of a diplomat.

I found myself in unfamiliar territory, extremely intrigued by her presence. My overreaction was evident as I felt my palms become sweaty. I found myself perspiring as if I was back in Ms. Johnson's fourth grade math class. *What is happening to me?* I thought. *Get a hold of yourself.*

Never had I felt so quickly and strongly the need to know another person. I was lightheaded. Unable to understand this weakness of mine, I remained frozen to my chair, trying to stay calm and disguise my reaction to her.

Then this beautiful woman moved closer to me and with a smile and another touch on the forearm, she leaned in, revealing the creamy skin of her legs. Her breath was of warm jasmine and her hair gleamed like the crystal chandeliers above as it slid off her shoulders, exposing her fragile build.

Her face touched my cheek lightly as she whispered into my right ear, "My friends call me Amanda. Can I just call you handsome?"

"I would just prefer if you used my name," I said, trying not to disclose the mild shaking I began to feel inside. "It's a pleasure to meet you." I said pulling back.

"I'm from up north," she said, "Portland originally, how about you?"

"From San Ramon," I replied.

Her smile was disarming, and her voice radiated kindness and understanding. In an instant, I felt at ease.

She said she had spent some time living in the East Bay, and we compared notes on a couple of our favorite restaurants. With each passing minute of hearing her speak, I continued to be hypnotized. There was something unusual in play. She projected comfort in a way that was unfamiliar to me, almost as if we already knew each other.

"Have we met somewhere before?" I asked.

"I don't believe I've had the pleasure, but it's been really nice meeting you now," she said. "I have a tendency to search out either the most sexual or intellectual man in a room, depending on my needs. Which one of those might you be?" she laughed lightly.

Outwardly, I chuckled, but inside I was momentarily terrified. Not of Amanda, but of my wife who by this time was staring attentively toward us from the other end of the stage. It took me a second to react with a smile and realize it may not be in my best interest to stay in the presence of this woman.

I turned away from Amanda and quickly changed my focus to the presentations on stage.

What is she doing to me, I asked myself. It felt as though

my free will was in the hands of this stranger. As if my mind had been hijacked and she could make me say or do anything she wanted, even becoming submissive and helpless to object.

Temporarily confused, I couldn't explain it. I continued to feel drawn to this woman with an internal feeling of peril. *I'm not weak, I'm happily married and in love*, I said to myself over and over, but a force was at work here that I had not encountered before.

Then, as if I hadn't sufficiently exposed myself to Amanda, my eyes suddenly watered and I began to feel deeply emotional. It was hard to breath, crushing, like I was suffocating from the inside. But she just stared straight ahead, like I didn't matter, I wanted to sob. It felt like she had gotten inside my head.

Gathering the few independent thoughts I had left, I turned to her: "There is something very commanding about you—I don't know any other way to describe it. I feel absorbed by you, as if you've breached my armor, leaving me exposed and unprotected. It's overpowering. How are you able to do it?" I asked holding back my tears.

"Could it be that I'm a sociopath," she said candidly in an off-handed way.

I let out a small laugh to acknowledge her joke. But, Amanda wore a strange grin. For a second, I remained silent and expressionless, waiting for the punch line. But it didn't come. Instead, Amanda remained focused on me, waiting for me to reply to her statement.

When I didn't speak, her blue eyes still hypnotizing now fixated on me, not waiting, but expecting, demanding a response. My unintentional wavering seemed to have complicated matters. I hadn't said anything on cue as I was supposed to. She was different now, absent and serious. I had broken something, a covenant of sorts.

Still struggling with my emotions, I began to feel weaker than before, as if anything I said would now be self-defeating, so I gave a crooked smile, as if to break the frozen moment.

"Are you serious?" I asked. "Why are you telling me this, Amanda?"

Her face instantly reverted back to a smile, projecting radiance and confidence.

"I'm bored with you and with this entire function. You and everyone here bore me," she sighed.

"Pardon me?" I replied feeling my heart sink.

"What does it matter if I reveal this to you? There's nothing you can do about it, and no one would believe you. I guess I wanted to spice things up a bit. I could tell you my life story and eat your fear like candy," she said, her voice cracking. In an instant I saw Amanda in another light. She was not the same person who had total control over me. Suddenly, she looked vulnerable. Then, just as quickly, as if someone in the next room had flipped a switch, it was gone.

Now, I believe, for that moment, she had revealed herself to me. But it came at a price because it broke her hold on me. Amanda looked weak and frail now.

There was new clarity in my perception of her. Her earlier statement of being a sociopath had cut me, but now I was no longer fooled by her charm and beauty. My body armor had closed and my guard was up.

"It's true. When I was 16, I was clinically diagnosed with antisocial personality disorder. I don't seem antisocial do I?" she asked calmly. "There are variations though, and apparently I'm the type who is more interested in money and power. I don't kill people, so don't worry. For the moment, you're safe, that is unless I'm threatened, or I want your job or your money, or I become obsessed with you. Then you're in trouble," she laughed.

"As for the power you recognize, handsome, it's real. I can control you and almost anyone else in some way, using subtle signals with my mind and body, if I wish. When you react, I counter it with a compliment or a gesture to set you at ease. I reassure you the entire time we are conversing without your knowing. I project your own ideas and behavior back to you so you find it recognizable and comforting," she said.

Silently, I sat still, feeling both dread and exhilaration.

I listened as her voice seemed to take on an arrogant tone.

"Can I imitate every emotion I need to? You bet, and better than most," she said. "I cry real tears, laugh at jokes, and know how to express more passion than the most passionate human being you know. When I have sex with a man, I may well show tears, giving them the impression I am crying with emotion. They tend to fall deeply in love with me every time. I can't get rid of them. That's real power," she exclaimed.

I heard contentment in her voice, as if she was reliving numerous experiences of her life in front of my eyes.

My own memorable experience with a sociopath was when my friend Gordon married his college girlfriend Emily, voted 'The Girl Most Likely To.' I laugh to myself when I think of that phrase and how appropriate it was for her. Emily had what was called an episode. I called it a meltdown. Emily was a twenty-two-year-old blonde beauty who had graduated from law school in Northern California in just two years. The school newspaper dubbed her "a superstar who literally set the bar" at her law school by attaining the highest grades of any graduate in the school's history. Highly intellectual, Emily didn't bend to anyone. Gordon admired that latter quality almost as much as he revered her body and mind. Emily had a cruel streak though, and was always on the defensive, blaming everyone else for any bad luck she experienced. This, in combination with her being a lawyer, made it increasingly arduous to control her actions.

From the beginning, Gordon knew Emily would be a successful lawyer, especially because she was a master manipulator. But Gordon, being who he was, had faith in their relationship and figured that in time her behavior would subside. Small things would occur that seemed like red flags to me; like when Gordon asked me to be his best man, Emily became furious. None of us could understand why. Of course, who was I to get in the way of fate and love? I reluctantly declined his offer to participate but I still showed up at the wedding to support my friend. She hinted to me, that she would hunt and kill me if I ever took Gordon away from her.

After the wedding, Emily decided she would stay home while Gordon continued working at his corporate job. I watched Gordon work long hours for three years to give Emily whatever she wanted, including a new car every year, monthly shopping sprees, and expensive jewelry. Then one day, he left me a message to call him immediately. He was frantic. A realtor he met for breakfast told him that almost a year earlier Emily had purchased a mid-sized home from him in Glendale, just over thirty minutes east of their home. Part of me was shocked for a second, then it quickly made sense because Emily was constantly misplacing expensive gifts Gordon would give her. No doubt she had turned those gifts into cash to pay for the home.

The realtor told Gordon, the other home was fully furnished and, worse, she had another man living there. Gordon picked me up within twenty minutes. I canceled my scheduled meetings and accompanied him to the address of the other home. When we arrived, we saw Emily at the doorway in the arms of the other man. Gordon was devastated. He opened his door, jumped out, and rushed up to Emily. When she saw him running toward her, she stopped and stared at him with a blank expression as if she didn't understand his reaction. She just stood there, like she was studying him. Gordon was in shock. I could see him on the verge of tears. I felt for him, but I stayed focused on Emily, waiting, silently begging for her to say something; then finally, after a minute, her lips moved. *We're done*, she told Gordon, then turned and walked away. Who does that after three years of marriage?

It turned out Emily was arrested a few months later and was forced by the court system to get help. Gordon called to tell me she was diagnosed as a sociopath while in the hospital. He still loved her after all she had put him through, and the last time we spoke, he was thinking of getting back with her. He often says that she had gotten into his head and he couldn't get her out. Emily always thought it was me who had told Gordon about her other house and boyfriend. The last words I remember Emily saying to me were, *I'm coming back for you.* I still get chills.

That story still haunts me, which is why Amanda's confession took me by surprise.

I turned my attention back to the event in front of me, content to say nothing more to Amanda. Though I was not in the least bit concerned for my safety, I found her to be a red flag like Emily and someone to stay away from.

As we sat quietly, I wondered if she was still controlling me, because a thread of curiosity kept pulling me back to her. *This could be an opportunity to learn how a sociopath lives*, I justified to myself. Besides, it's not every day someone comes up to you and divulges they are a sociopath, unless they really are a sociopath.

Finally, I turned to Amanda. "Are you hunting?" I blurted.

She chuckled, not in the least bit surprised. "I already have a target," she said. "Tonight I've planned an interesting evening for my gentleman friend. I need his help to get a promotion."

"This man can help you?" I asked.

"I will give him an experience he won't soon forget," she responded. "I'll open him up until I see his soul, make him fall in love with me, and then destroy his will to live. When I'm done with him, he'll be an empty shell."

"Why are you doing this?" I asked, bluntly.

"I already told you," she responded, "I'm bored. I'll destroy him and anyone who gets in my way."

I quivered at her lack of emotion and at her matter of fact demeanor. She seemed so ruthless. Even with her confession, I couldn't look away. I could still feel her blue eyes pulling me toward her, like a piece of nylon string around my neck. It was as if I was caught in a web excited to be eaten by the spider. She was just too powerful.

I remained at my chair, straight-faced and motionless. Gradually sipping my wine, I continued to listen to Amanda over the next forty-five minutes or so, standing on cue to applaud the ceremony up to the serving of the coffee.

In the end, the event turned out to be quite a thrill for me. I could not have predicted I'd have met Amanda on a night I thought would be uninteresting.

At the end of the evening my wife, along with Amanda's friend, briefly joined us at the table for a nightcap. After congratulations were given, we went our separate ways. I hesitated to inform the gentlemen of his upcoming adventure.

The next week, I arrived for my daily cup at my favorite coffee shop. A place I frequent to work on my latest novel. I couldn't escape the familiar sweet smell of jasmine perfume that seemed to permeate around me. When I looked up, there she stood at the edge of the table, just as lovely as I'd remembered.

"May I sit down," she asked. "I wasn't finished talking with you last week."

"Please sit down," I said, "Am I your next target Amanda?"

"No," she said, "I just needed someone to talk to."

"I am here every other day, you're welcome anytime," I said.

I wasn't alarmed or concerned anymore that I could be manipulated or fooled. I had already felt her power, so I was content to just listen.

From that day forward, Amanda would show up every other day. Most of the time, I never said a word but she never disappointed me. She would be what I came to call quintessential Amanda: high-class fashion plate, breathless and brimming with a kind of urgency to describe her past experiences at times referring to her private diary. Progressively, the stories from the visits began to develop a pattern

I can only describe as a life of doorways. Each led to a path that would take Amanda to a higher rung on a social ladder, but only by means of lies, manipulations, and usually sex. She acknowledged men she wore as if they were a badge of honor. But there was ultimately destruction and desperation at the end of each path, and so it was on to the next doorway, always hunting.

On the next visit, Amanda didn't show.

CHAPTER 1

MOMENTS OF TRUTH

I WAS THIRTEEN AND THOMAS WAS FOURTEEN. EVERYONE AT school knew him. Intelligent, popular and good-looking. His dark blonde hair complimented those perfect green eyes and high cheekbones. People noticed me when I was standing next to him at school; otherwise, I was invisible. Who looks at a pale, skinny blonde with braces? But Thomas was different; he paid attention to me. When I was with him, I got the attention I deserved.

Lucky for me, Thomas didn't live far, so he and I rode the same bus to school and got off at the same stop. If it wasn't for him, I'm not sure I could have continued in school. I couldn't keep friends. And some of the girls had started a rumor that I was rude and snobby.

That bothered me until I started to eye Thomas. He and I usually sat together. Sometimes, I would catch him staring at my face and lips and even my breasts. I learned early, even at thirteen, that guys wanted to touch me. Contrary to Mother's opinion, I was good for something after all. *Guys want me, even if you don't, Mother*, I told myself. I didn't have much of a figure yet, but Thomas was curious, and he would get embarrassed when I caught him looking. I knew it was his weakness. Some days I would wear a short skirt under my pants so Mother wouldn't see. When I got to school I would take off my pants so Thomas could see my legs. His eyes would look crazy at me. I felt powerful, like I was controlling him.

Of course I wanted Thomas all to myself, but Sandy was my competition. She would wait for him, always wearing one of her slutty dresses and high heels. Sandy was upscale, her parents had lots of money, and she was the most popular girl in school, with her eyes on Thomas. She was smart and I knew she wouldn't go down easily. I could see why Thomas was attracted to her. She wore red lipstick; it was so luscious that, in a weird way, I admired her too.

Sandy had that arrogant swagger that I couldn't compete with, but there was something else. I knew Thomas was curious about sex, and she knew it too. I told myself that I probably wouldn't have to go all the way, just enough to satisfy his crazy curious hormones. I swear, there were times when I was around Thomas I could smell his hormones peaking.

I just needed a little more time to establish my popularity.

Without much thought of any consequences, I made Sandy my target. I couldn't help myself; she remained on my mind. I had to remove her from the equation. It was the only way to get more time with Thomas.

The opportunity came one day when I searched my

parents' room and found a box of condoms. It was easy for me to take one and place it in Sandy's desk so everyone could see it, but it had to be at a perfect time, when the classroom was full.

Just before lunch, I turned to Sandy and asked if I could borrow a pencil. When she raised the top of her desk, the condom fell to the floor. Everyone shrieked. I still remember the look on her face, it was priceless. With all the drama that followed, my Sandy problem was solved and I had Thomas all to myself.

The stop at the end of the day for Thomas and me was my opportunity. He was still getting off when I looked back at the bus. I slowly skipped down the sidewalk onto a trail leading into a wooded area.

Thomas was right behind me.

"Where are you going Amanda?" he asked.

When I abruptly stopped and turned around, Thomas bumped right up against me, face to face. He looked at me with those beautiful, hungry green eyes.

"What are you doing?" he asked.

"Wouldn't you like to touch me Thomas?" I asked. "I know you like me."

I could feel him trembling, and although the look on his face was eager, he held back.

"I want to, but I don't know for sure," he said.

"Would you like to touch me?" I whispered. "To taste me?" I moved closer, until his body touched mine. I felt it.

He wanted me.

Finally, he pulled me to him. I could feel his desire for me. This time, he moved his left hand to my breast.

It was awkward but I didn't care. I liked it. I'll let whoever I want touch me. *I do what I want when I want with whomever I want*, I told myself.

His right hand moved to the back of my neck. First he kissed me on my cheek. He smelled like sweet coconut. It was his dad's cologne. I liked Mr. Armour; he let us call him by his first name: Dean. Dean was a handsome man for thirty-five.

Thomas moved slowly toward my mouth until his soft lips found mine. The taste of cherries from my lipstick became stronger and I could feel his breath against mine. Thomas kept pulling me tighter. His hand moved under my blouse. I took a breath as the kissing became more aggressive. I waited.

I opened my eyes and saw his were closed. I was confused. Then his tongue went deep into my mouth. I looked up toward the top of the trees and then down to the ground, but there were no butterflies in my stomach. I still waited.

After a moment, nothing, just slobber. I didn't feel anything, just empty, with the taste of my cherry lipstick. I was tired of waiting.

My mind was upset. Aunt Dorothy said the first kiss is a wonderful feeling and you get butterflies and excited. Unforgettable—stuff like that.

I blamed Thomas. He was too slow and clumsy. I was impatient, so I pulled him to me and we kissed more deeply on the lips. But it was even worse. This time it reminded me of the taste of metal in my mouth. Yuck.

I went for a third try. I placed my right arm at the back of his neck and pulled him to me. After two more seconds, our lips separated. Nothing! I felt jilted. I had done everything right, so it had to be Thomas's fault; he was doing something wrong.

"Get away," I said, "or I'll tell everyone you forced me to do it." Thomas turned and started running away toward his house down the sidewalk. Something in my head seemed to take control; I didn't know what came over me. I almost couldn't control myself. I wanted to hurt him for the disappointment I felt.

My mind had already decided I was wronged. I was the victim and I should take action. Within seconds, I made a decision to handle it on Monday at school. I buttoned up my blouse and skipped home to finish my homework.

Over the weekend, the experience with Thomas began replaying over and over in my mind. It was impossible to stop. Every time I closed my eyes, I was watching Thomas become aroused. The thought exploded my senses. My brain memorized every small detail. As if a switch had been turned on, my senses became enhanced, awakened. The change in Thomas's chemistry—the fear—that was the high for me.

But, I was also amazed at something else. I smelled his body produce a hormonal scent, as an animal would. I could even taste it on my tongue. When his breathing grew rapid, it sounded like a loud bell in my head, with each heartbeat louder than the one before, even though I was feet away; I had to breathe it in. He had no idea what was happening to him but I was able to sense it all.

It was me, I did it, I thought to myself. *I can make people do things, like a god.* The look in his eyes told me he would have done anything for me at that moment and I never forgot that.

When Monday came, I told Jen, a girl at school, that Thomas forced me to kiss him and had also touched me. At the time, I didn't realize it would be such a big deal, but apparently someone told the principal. By nine o'clock I was in the principal's office where I was met by my parents looking as if something terribly wrong had happened. Daddy hugged me. Mother stared at me with a look of disappointment, as if to say, *I know you're evil.*

It was the same glare she gave me when her dog Scully died. It happened when I was nine. Mother had to leave a lecture she was giving at the university and cried for days. The veterinarian said Scully had been poisoned with the same sleeping pills Mother was taking. Nobody could figure out how it happened. I thought Mother gave Scully way too much attention anyway. I guess she blamed me for what happened to Scully.

"Amanda, is it true a boy here in this school forced you to kiss him?" Principal Fredericks asked. "I need for you to tell me the truth."

They were hovering over me. I had already said that he did. I would look bad if I denied it, especially in front of my parents. *Besides, I'm the victim*, I thought. *He took advantage of me.* I saw the look on his face when he was touching and kissing me. His eyes reminded me of Mr. Allen's from Daddy's lodge night. Mr. Allen always licked his lips when he saw me; it had made me sick.

"It was Thomas, Ms. Fredericks," I said. "He did it, he made me kiss him."

I looked at Mother; her eyes became teary. Daddy looked angry. He took Principal Fredericks aside and they had what seemed to be a serious discussion. The next day, Thomas was gone. I heard he was punished and sent to a detention facility.

I did it. I controlled everyone, including Daddy and the principal. Thomas was taken to a detention facility because of me. Now I felt as though I could do anything.

CHAPTER 2

SHEEP OR WOLF

SHORTLY AFTER THE INCIDENT WITH THOMAS, DADDY announced he was taking a new job and we would be moving a short ways outside Portland to a small town called Happy Valley. Mother received a waiver for me to graduate seventh grade early, so we could leave a month before the school year ended. Within three days the movers came, packed, and cleared out our house. They did it without telling me or my brother, Jamie. He cried because there was no chance to say goodbye to his friends. I didn't care. I knew Mother was behind it all and didn't trust me, and I didn't have any real friends to say goodbye to anyway. I do have to say though, that I gave my parents credit because they were usually so predictable, and they pulled off the move so suddenly and completely that it took me by surprise. I didn't see that one coming.

It only took about a half hour to get to Happy Valley. Our new house was a beautiful white two-story, with red brick along the lower part of the foundation. The house sat almost a hundred feet from the edge of a paved circle driveway surrounded by large trees. The front lawn was plush green, and there were flowerboxes under the windowsills. Up the wooden stairs were two large bedrooms. Mine had two spacious closets for all my clothes and shoes. The three-car garage was large enough to park Mother's Volvo and Daddy's Mercedes, instead of one stall like at the old house. When Daddy wasn't traveling, he would be able to enjoy his hobby of working on model trains. I heard Mother say she was going to set up her art studio in the guest quarters off to the east side of the house.

Our neighborhood was close to Ashley Meadows, a park with a network of walking trails where my parents said we would be able to play and exercise. The town was small but had lots of greenery. I felt I could actually breathe, not like in Portland, where we had nosy people around us.

The view out my bedroom window was great. I could see a large green lawn in the distance and some neighborhood kids playing on the corner. It seemed lively, and since my parents made friends easily, it wouldn't be long before Mother was making her famous granola, welcoming them over. I predicted that soon all the parents would be sharing duties and taking turns carpooling to soccer and baseball games. Mother had to be proud of herself, I thought. She had managed to recreate our quaint lifestyle.

Organizing the house was exhausting. Each of us helped bring boxes up to our rooms. Mother still looked at me in that way of hers. It was like a chess game with us: she would make a move, and then I would. I kept an eye on her every day, but she never gave me more than a hint. Maybe she was trying to forget the Thomas incident, hoping thoughts of him would disappear amid new surroundings. A few months later, when my fourteenth birthday came and went without much acknowledgment, I blamed it on the move, but didn't say anything. Besides, it wouldn't have made a difference. Mother and I didn't trust each other; she knew I was watching her, wondering what she was up to.

My introduction to the first day of eighth grade left me with a sense that Mother definitely had an agenda. With the various academic and sporting requirements, it would be difficult for me to find time to be alone. Keep me busy—that was Mother's plan. I wanted to sit down with her and talk like an adult. Tell her I was different and that I just needed some time to figure things out. But she would never understand. She didn't know it was vital for me to be alone. Private time usually helped me to process all the information coming at me. I needed to compartmentalize, to access what I needed when I needed it.

On the First day of school, I met Sara. Sara was fourteen like me. She, her younger brother, and her mom and dad had moved in across the street. They moved from Bakersfield to be closer to the country.

When our teacher introduced Sara to the class, a part of me observed she was emotional, or an empath, as I like to call them. Only because her eyes watered when she described how sad it was to leave their home and friends behind. Sara told the class she especially missed her friend Patty. Sara was exactly what I needed and convenient because she lived across the street from me. She was perfect for me to mold. *If I can keep her around*, I thought, *I won't seem odd like I did at the other school, where I didn't have the appearance of having a single friend.* The very same day after school, across the way, I could see Sara upstairs organizing her room. She saw me too. It turned out we could see each others' upstairs rooms from across the street.

Within a few days, I learned from Mother that Sara collected precious stones. I managed to take a couple diamonds off from some of Mother's jewelry and I gave them to Sara as a welcome present to the neighborhood. She didn't like me at first and looked away, but when she saw they were real diamonds, she gave in.

To describe Sara would be to use the definition of average. Always wearing the same colors - blacks mixed with browns and blues - along with having uncombed auburn hair. Her pale skin needed some work, and since she was late physically developing, she lacked confidence. So I decided I'd build her up. Tell her how pretty she was. I'd pretend to be like a sheep—that's how I saw her—while I got the advantage of looking "normal" to others, like Mother.

Sara and I became friends, as far as that goes for me. Later, we even had telescopes and we would watch each other across the drive, communicating using sign language we learned in class.

But Sara was emotionally high maintenance. She had a desperate need to be acknowledged. Between keeping up her confidence, completing my schoolwork and all the activities, I was exhausted. Mother's plan was in high gear and working well.

Sara's mom, Mari, was forty-something, with a huge head of fake bleached blonde hair, and louder than a bunch of women at a lingerie party. She also had a successful practice as a psychiatrist, with a list of clients that included famous movie stars and CEO's of large companies. Sara said they used to go to their house in Bakersfield, and since her reputation was so good, they were now coming all the way to Happy Valley just to meet with her. Sara mentioned to me one day that she had actually hid under a desk in her mother's office to listen in on a patient's session. She said her mother used a ritual on the patient that she wanted us to try sometime.

Prior to them moving in, Mother and I met Mari in their yard when she began the design phase to construct her office. The finished product was a stunning sight, complete with hardwood floors and red mahogany siding. It was attached to the main structure, but also had its own entrance. It resembled a cute, serene Victorian lake house.

Sara's parents, Mr. and Mrs. Rousseau, became good friends with mine. Mari Rousseau was tall like Mother and both of them had blonde hair, even if Mari's was out of a bottle. From behind, they kind of looked like sisters. Mr.

Rousseau was soft spoken with a strong French accent. He and Daddy enjoyed playing poker on Friday nights, and spent a lot of Saturdays talking about the stock market. Daddy and my little brother went on camping trips with Mr. Rousseau and Sara's little brother, Lee. Mother and Mrs. Rousseau liked to shop together, usually on Saturday afternoons. Sara and I worked on school stuff a lot of the time and even shared our turning-fifteen birthdays. Sara gave the appearance I was fitting in, and Mother seemed to be satisfied I was adjusting and not causing problems.

One day Sara became insistent that we use the ritual she learned from her mother's patient session. "Let's do it," she said, "it'll cement our friendship." Being the empath she was, Sara found me to be a challenge, and felt destined to help everyone she thought was troubled. This weakness would open her up to me over and over again. But, right now, I needed her too, and admittedly, I was curious.

"It won't hurt," she insisted, "and I changed it so it'll work for us and we'll be friends forever." She said it was important to conduct it at exactly six p.m., the same time her mom used it on the patient. We scheduled it for the next day in Sara's room on Wednesday, after school.

The first thing in the morning, Sara reminded me of our six p.m. appointment. I liked the fact she was energized about something. I was mainly curious about the type of methods a psychotherapist used on patients, so at the time, it had a meaning for me. When we arrived home, Sara came running over to my house to inform me the ritual consisted of three phases and we had to follow them exactly. She invited me back to her room where we wouldn't be disturbed.

When the clock struck the appropriate time, there I was sitting across from Sara. She was holding my hands and I was holding hers and we were looking into each other's eyes.

Sara blurted. "Repeat after me: 'I am a confident person and I will not have sex with men for the feeling of being held.'"

"What?" I said surprised. "We're too young to have sex with men, Sara," I said.

"We have to say it Amanda. If we don't, we won't be friends forever," she responded.

"The words are not appropriate Sara," I insisted.

When I looked at her face again, her chin began an odd shaking and she was starting to look pathetic.

"Okay, I'll do it," I said quickly.

After it was over, Sara stayed quiet as if meditating to the words. I guessed she was following the actions her mother took with the patient as exactly as she could.

I figured Sara's mother, Mari, was probably helping her patient overcome an addiction to men, or sex, or both. Her method of psychotherapy, I thought, was simple enough, and since Mari was successful with her practice, it might somehow help me. So I recited every word exactly as Sara had requested, and she did the same.

I thought it was odd that there was nothing in the ritual about friendship and being friends. But I didn't say anything;

I didn't want to see that awful expression on Sara's face again. *How do people do it? It's a lot of work to be normal,* I thought.

When we were done, Sara hugged me. "I love you, Amanda," she said. "We'll be friends forever now."

I paused for a second, not understanding what I should say. I repeated the very words she said to me: "I love you, Sara, and we'll be friends forever."

When I turned to leave, Sara's look caught me by surprise. There were tears streaming down her face. They looked sparkly. Then she said it again, "I love you, Amanda," and walked away. Why didn't I have tears on my face? My mind flashed for a second to when I saw Daddy wiping tears from Mother's eyes when Grandpa died. *What is the significance of tears?* I wondered.

Daddy would get tears too. He would sit us in a circle and discuss how we could be more considerate of Mother's feelings. My little brother would cry and I would just sit there. Sometimes I rubbed my eyes, so it looked like I was crying too.

Jamie actually asked me one time, "Why don't you ever cry, Amanda?" At first, I disregarded the question, but then later I began to think more about it and he was right. When I was punished for not completing my chores, it bothered me to have to sit in my room, but I didn't cry or care if Mother would cry about it or if somebody else would have to do them instead of me. It just seemed like Mother was pathetic, and I wasn't weak like her.

EYES OF A SOCIOPATH

It was then I came to realize something about Sara. The entire ritual thing was her subconscious telling her something in me was missing and I needed help. Was it the crying thing? I knew I was different. Was she trying to help me but didn't know it? Or was it instinctual? Either way, I had invested a lot of time in Sara and I didn't have time to train someone else. So whatever. It seemed minor to go along with something of hers every now and then.

Sara would always bring up ideas to entertain us. On one occasion she suggested we set up a string across the road, put notes on it and then pull from her room to mine, and each day, she would send me one and I would do the same. Then she came up with the idea of us listening in on some of her mother's patients' sessions.

"We can place a recorder in my mother's office and listen to their juicy stories; it'll be fun," she said. "We can hear my mom helping the man who dresses like a woman. It's a big secret. He's some big movie star or something."

I didn't buy into it until Sara brought me the recorder she had placed in her mom's office with a patient talking. I was fascinated by the stories. Sara made a plan to collect the recordings at the end of each day. We sat and listened to the sessions during the evenings. During one of them, Mari was treating a lady who would have visions of her dead mother living somewhere else with another family. It seemed she was unable to accept her death. Another was of a doctor who couldn't get past losing a child on the operating table, blaming himself for the death. There were several but I bₑ especially interested in a patient named Kathryn, a woman Mari was treating weekly who was a sociopath. Sara would bring me the recordings of Kathryn's visits. I'd take them home and listen to them privately.

Kathryn was a thirty-eight-year-old woman who had become sex-obsessed. She used sex to get job promotions, trips, expensive dinners and jewelry. Mari was working with her because Kathryn couldn't say no to men who would pay attention to her. Kathryn would fly around the world to meet men and whore herself out. Excluding the sex part, I began to see something similar between my condition and Kathryn's. We shared the ability to read people, study their weaknesses, and target those who we thought were a threat to us. She was even having strange dreams like me. Kathryn had been abused as a child and it seemed to Mari the abuse could have contributed to her problems. Well, Mother was always suspicious of me. She could be rude and cold to me. Maybe that "abuse" made me how I was, I thought to myself. The more I listened to the descriptions of Kathryn's symptoms, the more it could have been me she was talking about. Mari's next session with Kathryn was about having a lack of emotion and concern for other people.

I never mentioned this stuff to anyone. Kathryn and I were similar, but I was much smarter; I knew I wouldn't get caught up in a mess like she did. I became concerned about how to control what was happening to me, or what I was

.idn't know everything about myself like I
.aght.

, that some of the symptoms we share could
.ito aggressive behavior toward others. It was
im͜ .it for me to understand the difference between
reality and perceived situations, so I wouldn't target people
for just about anything. Threatening behavior, judgment, and
envy were a large part of Kathryn's issues that I also shared.
I had to admit to myself, I fit her profile and these were the
things Mari was trying to change.

I continued to listen to Kathryn's sessions for several
months and realized I needed more practice to fit in. I needed
Sara's help so I told her I wanted to be an actress one day. She
helped me rehearse how I needed to act in situations when
communicating with people, how to laugh, be sad, cry, and
be concerned. Kathryn had learned to cry if she was ever
cornered or caught lying. According to Kathryn, people felt
sorry for you, and using pity was a distraction. She thought of
it as the key to her becoming functional. It was also necessary
to use tears if an animal or human dies. So Sara and I focused
on me crying believably.

The problem was that I was not always quick enough
to recall what to say or do. I had to look at the situation
and pause, think about it, before giving the proper response.
But, my working with Sara improved everything about me.
It changed the entire way Mother and Daddy would relate
to me. It was like I learned a new language. Even when they

noticed that I did pause, if I came up with

tion, they smiled. We actually played and la

for the first time. It opened up a new world.

Listening to Kathryn's sessions became signi

I learned three important things:

First, I did not meet the criteria of being a serial killer.

Second, pity is my friend and will protect me when I'm cornered.

Third, to get whatever I want, use the words, "I Love You."

At sixteen, it all began to come together for me.

CHAPTER 3

DIAGNOSIS: ARMED
AND DANGEROUS

IN SPITE OF MY OCCASIONALLY GETTING IN TROUBLE, IT WAS difficult for my parents to question my perfect grade point average and attendance. Plus, I exceeded the high school standards in math and critical thinking, and scored 2100 on the SAT, placing me in the 90th percentile. My teachers all encouraged Mother to get my IQ tested so I could get gifted services, but she never did.

I attributed my improvement to the patient sessions between Mari and Kathryn.

Not knowing why, I was changing in other ways too. It seemed as though my mind continued assessing everyone around me to see how far I could control them. So even with my better communication skills, my behavior started wearing on my parents again. Although I was already sixteen, Mother insisted she approve my every outfit because my clothes, as she described them, left little to the imagination. Of course, with some tape, I was creative enough to alter them once I got to school to reflect my fashion sense and showcase my assets. Sneaking a boy up to my room late at night from time to time also gave them worry. I would let them touch me, but I didn't give in to sex.

My arrest for shoplifting was a low point for my parents. It didn't faze me, however. It was just one small glimmering red lipstick. Since when are the police called for a five-dollar lipstick? If it had been a man who caught me, I could have just yelled, "he touched me" and gotten away with it. But this time it was a woman officer.

I was grounded for a week. I heard my parents whispering to each other that I could be sent away to a correctional school, even for a first offense. I panicked. *What if they put me in with Thomas? He would surely kill me*, I thought. But then I remembered he was dumb and I was a lot smarter than him. I was more afraid of being beaten and sexually assaulted by others, and what if there were needles? I am deathly afraid of needles.

The next day, my parents met with me to explain that the court was forcing me to get treatment, or go to jail. Also, if I got into trouble within a year after that, the charge would be reinstated. It was important for me to follow the judge's order, they said. I agreed we had to keep me away from jail.

A week later, there was a crisis at our school. Wesley, a boy in my math class, had some kind of an incident. I knew him only because his eyes were almost black and I liked to stare at him. He would catch me all the time. Something about his eyes intrigued me, and besides, he had a beautiful face for a boy.

Actually, I thought Wesley deserved what he got. He bothered me. Luckily none of the other kids knew how I felt about him, not even Sara. Still, my parents and I got dragged into it.

The intercom came on during math class: *Amanda Preston, please report to Principal Beckman's office.* Sara and the other students in the class looked at me as if I had murdered one of their family members. I joined Mother and Daddy, who were already present. Daddy had that same blank stare as usual and Mother was moving about in her nervous way, just like when we had to see Principal Fredericks about Thomas. Mother explained that Principal Beckman had some questions for me.

"Amanda, do you know Wesley?" Principal Beckman asked.

Of course I do, I thought to myself.

"I know Wesley from class. He's the boy with the dark eyes," I said staring out the glass into the clouded sky.

Suddenly, a clap of thunder struck loudly, reverberating against the building. I jumped up startled and rushed over to Daddy. The lights began flickering. For a moment, it felt as if the entire building had shaken off its foundation. Within seconds, the sky turned dark gray. Blowing rain and leaves pelted the large glass windows.

"Did you ever speak to him?" Principal Beckman asked, visibly shaken by the rumbling.

"We never really talk. He's very quiet, and I sit behind him in class. I imagine his eyes because they're so beautiful," I said. "Is there something wrong?"

"No, Amanda, it's fine," Principal Beckman replied. "I can see you have an excellent grade point average and you're a wonderful student. Keep up the good work. I apologize for bringing you all here. Have a good day. Amanda, you can go home now," she said.

Daddy hugged me. "Good girl, Amanda," he said as he hurried out. Mother and I walked swiftly down the hallway out to the parking lot. Neither of us spoke a word getting into the car.

The drive home led me to believe something was seriously wrong.

"What's happened?" I asked.

Mother looked straight ahead, seeming entranced by the rain pummeling the windshield.

She wouldn't respond to me. She stayed quiet while the wiper blades of the car moved loudly from side to side as if angered by the rain. *Okay, I'll play your little game, Mother,* I said to myself.

I asked again. "Did something happen to Wesley? Is he hurt?"

Mother's tears began rolling down her cheeks.

Still looking straight ahead, she asked, her voice shaking, "Do you remember Thomas a couple of years ago?"

"Yes, Mother, I remember."

"I want you to tell me what really happened. No more lies, no more games, Amanda."

"What are you talking about?" I asked.

Mother must have made the connection between what I did to Thomas and now she wanted me to admit to what I did to Wesley.

"You know what I'm talking about!" she shouted.

Was I on the witness stand accused of a heinous crime in front of a judge? I didn't like it. Her tone was threatening. *I can't believe I have to put up with this*, I thought.

The weather had worsened and visibility was poor. Mother slowed the car. I could tell she was struggling to stay focused on the roadway. The thunder and loud pounding sounded like rocks were battering the metal. I began to worry that we'd get into an accident. But Mother was determined to get an answer to her question.

"Amanda, you have pushed me too far. I know you better than you think," she said.

I lowered my head slightly, rubbing my eyes, remembering what I had learned from Kathryn. Mother was trying to corner me, so I began sniffling and crying. My face and eyes were red just like I wanted.

When I looked up at her, Mother looked fragile; she was breaking. I could sense it from her breathing and clammy skin. Suddenly a loud wail I had never heard before burst out of her. As if unable to catch her breath, she began choking.

I knew what she wanted; she wanted the truth.

"What happened with Thomas?!" she yelled.

"I told him to kiss me, and there were no butterflies or anything, Mother."

"What are you talking about Amanda?"

"Everybody said there would be butterflies and there wasn't. He deserved to be punished."

"Oh my, Amanda, you made up a story…because there were no butterflies?"

"Yes."

"Do you realize Thomas will probably be hurt for a long time from the lie you made up?"

"Yes," I replied.

"Help me, God. Help me," she said softly to herself, over and over.

I had underestimated her; she knew about me, she had figured me out. But when?

Still, it wasn't logical for her to have this much concern over an incident involving a boy she didn't know, I thought.

Struggling to breathe, Mother turned to me. "Wesley was struck by a moving car earlier this morning. He is badly hurt."

Without thinking, "Was he pushed, Mother?" I asked, unintentionally displaying my hand.

Mother, being my most adversarial opponent, let her emotions get in the way and didn't catch it. Sobbing and wiping her eyes, she explained, "You were seen talking to him, Amanda, just before it happened. A couple people say you were standing next to him by the street where he was run over. They saw you both walking together, and even though nobody saw what actually happened after that, the authorities suspect that Wesley was pushed into traffic."

"I didn't do it, Mother," I said. "It must have been somebody else, or maybe he tripped. You believe me, don't you?" I pleaded.

Mother didn't respond. Even though she was the one person I couldn't read, her expression seemed different.

The rain never let up even after we arrived home. Mother drove into the garage abruptly stopping inches from Daddy's tools. As if in a robotic state, she turned off the engine, stepped out and walked inside the house without speaking a word.

I raced upstairs and sat in my room. I listened to the rain as it fell onto the roof gutters, making a pinging noise. Mother knew what only a mother could about her child from pure instinct. For a split second, she had seen me as a weak child as I pleaded with her to believe me. What she didn't know was that moment would never come again. My senses were fully trained now, and Mother would not be able to catch another glimpse of the real me, no matter how in tuned she thought she was and how much she tried searching my face and actions.

As I figured, Mother didn't say a word to Daddy about her suspicions of me. Mother told me once, "Sometimes you remind me of your father." From the way she said it, I could tell it wasn't in a good way. She did her best to keep me away from him. She watched me incessantly, but I also watched her, waiting for clues to figure out her next move. I knew she had a plan that she would try and keep from me until she was good and ready.

When summer came, Daddy announced we would be leaving for a weeklong vacation in Hawaii. He had been spending a lot of time working toward tenure as a Science Professor at the University and wanted to make up for being away all the time. Daddy and I got along well; he didn't judge me like Mother did, and I can't say I really cared about anyone except for him, that is, if caring means I didn't want him to get hurt. Daddy loved me and I didn't like to see him sad. I gave him as much of what I thought of as love and emotion as I could. I was a good daughter, even if Mother didn't see that.

Our early flight on a Friday morning had us in Honolulu by lunchtime. We arrived at the Hawaiian Village, a huge resort surrounded by coconut trees. The temperature was a perfect eighty degrees with a slight breeze that brushed the side of my face when I stepped out of the car. I walked out to the shore to touch the turquoise blue water. For a moment, my mind wandered in a dream of meeting an island millionaire who would charm me away to a life away from Mother.

There was no idle time. By the end of the third day, we had gone scuba diving, played two rounds of golf, and visited the USS Arizona Memorial at Pearl Harbor. Though not much of a history buff, I thought it was pretty interesting to learn about battleships, destroyers and carriers during the war. I imagined myself as a large battleship calculating every move, maneuvering wherever I wanted, fighting against the world, destroying those around me. After the tour, we returned to the hotel. I sat on the beach and gazed into the distance. I was comatose; I needed stimulation. My brain was bored. And still, Mother watched me, trying to study me, while keeping everything that happened from Daddy.

I managed to control myself throughout the trip, getting along with my little brother most of the time. I was really tempted to hurt him once or twice, for my own stimulation and excitement, but I stopped myself.

CHAPTER 4

YOUR DAUGHTER IS A SOCIOPATH

ONE MORNING EARLY IN THE NEXT SCHOOL YEAR MOTHER told me I would be missing school for the whole day. She had scheduled an appointment for me to see a clinical psychologist in the valley.

Oh, yeah, I thought, *the stupid shoplifting charge.*

"I want you to be honest with Dr. Devereau today, Amanda," she said.

"I will, Mother."

"You have to tell her everything about Thomas and Wesley."

"I will, Mother."

"We have to find out what is happening, because if we don't, I'll lose my mind."

Mother quietly began her display of tears.

It wasn't far from our home, a little ways off the highway on Sunnyhill Street, not the traditional office where one might expect a doctor's office to be. It had a wonderful view of much of the city, and dogwoods, beautifully white in bloom, lined the driveway. Definitely an upscale neighborhood. I noticed different models of BMW's and a red Ferrari parked in neighboring driveways. The feel reminded me of Sara's mom's office and, like Mari, anyone who reached this level of success had to be good at what they did.

There were two parking spaces: one reserved for Dr. Devereau and the other for guests. Getting out of the car, I smelled the pungent aroma of sunflowers growing on the north side of the porch. When I turned, I was surprised at how large they were. There were some colorful objects scattered around the front lawn, which was a bit incongruous with the upscale image: a few pink flamingos, a blue statue of a frog on a lily pad, and a marble bust of a woman with medium-sized breasts, all of which I figured were there to give the impression she was open-minded to gay and lesbian couples or may be one herself. Walking the path to the door, I imagined Dr. Devereau as an independent middle-aged woman with a funky bent.

Closer to the front door, we saw an arrow directing us to the right, to a small asphalt island where we saw a knee-high ashtray mounted into a concrete pad. The webs on the doorframe and outside table gave me the idea she probably kept her money close and didn't trust too many people, a useless piece of information I recalled from a television program.

For a brief moment, my senses warned me about the visit but I didn't know why. I reminded myself it was a simple meeting to abide by the court order. Besides, I learned from Kathryn's sessions how to easily fool a doctor and get a normal diagnosis.

We were met at the door by Dr. Patricia Devereau.

"Hello, Mrs. Preston. Hello, Amanda," she said, in a strong French accent.

Wow. My eyes widened. This woman was beautiful. She had amazing green eyes, like jade, and her dark hair was shiny and looked polished. She was wearing Jimmy Choo light green, high-heeled sandals and her green shimmery eyeshadow was perfectly applied. She was captivating in the highest fashion sense; tall and potentially intimidating, but her beauty and her smile were completely effortless and relaxed.

"Welcome to my home. I hope you find it warm and enjoyable," she said.

Mother didn't sit; instead she walked over to me and explained she needed to run some errands. "See you in an hour," she said.

Dr. Devereau sat at her desk and crossed her legs. I hadn't figured I would be attracted to a woman, but I was clearly looking at her long legs. Not wasting any time, she dug right in.

"So, Amanda, I understand your visit here today is a requirement of the judge to satisfy a claim of shoplifting. Is this correct?"

"Yes, Dr. Devereau, it is. But it didn't happen the way they said."

"Tell me what happened."

"I saw a tube of lipstick; it was on the floor at Macy's. I was just picking it up and I guess I accidentally put it in my purse."

"What kind was it, Amanda?"

"I'm not sure, just a little shiny gold tube of red lipstick."

"Well, it doesn't sound so serious to me for a sixteen-year-old, Amanda. I took an entire lipstick set from a store once when I was fifteen, and look at me: I think I turned out okay. It's a normal thing," Dr. Devereau said, smiling.

She called me normal. It set me at ease. I didn't see a need to be defensive. I leaned back, crossing my legs to relax.

Dr. Devereau was the happy psychologist, someone to help me get through the process so we could both move on. *Someone give her the $100 and let's go home*, I thought to myself.

"Do your friends also wear makeup?" she asked.

She wasn't being accusatory toward me, and she assumed I had friends. This made her easy to talk to, so I answered.

"No, Sara doesn't wear makeup. We've been friends for two years now."

"When I was growing up, Amanda, I didn't have many friends either. I kind of liked being alone so I could use my imagination and explore more of what my mind could do."

Immediately, my guard went up. Before I consciously realized it, my mind recognized that she implied I didn't have many friends. I didn't exactly say that. Her assumption might have been based on information provided to her from someone else, or maybe it was a leap on her part. Immediately her tone and body movement changed ever so slightly along with her facial expression, indicating to me she wasn't sure. Dr. Devereau was good, but I was better.

She stood up and looked away, trying to create a distraction, hoping to recover. She didn't fool me. I was careful not to change my posture, except to glance for a second at the wind chimes outside her window. I purposely did it to give her an opportunity to reassess her method.

"Amanda, are you sexually active?"

Without hesitation, I responded, "No, Dr. Devereau, I'm a virgin."

"You're a charming, beautiful girl. You probably get a lot of attention. I'm sure you've already experienced boys calling you."

"Not really," I replied.

Dr. Devereau had complimented me again. I liked it. She had said I was beautiful and normal. Maybe her earlier slip was just that; but I thought I would be cautious with her, so I didn't respond further.

"We don't have a lot of time, Amanda, so tell me a little bit about you. What kind of brain do you have?"

I was intrigued. Instead of asking me what pets or hobbies I had, she asked me a logical question. It made total sense, to take an inventory of my brain. I was eager to reply.

"I have an excellent memory, Dr. Devereau. I tested it, like how many times I wore red on Sundays since I was ten years old to now at sixteen. I counted four times. I also practice math problems, science, arts and languages, measuring how many words I can retain."

"I think you are one of the most charming patients I have ever had, Amanda. Are there any particular questions you would like to ask of me at this session today?" she asked.

I didn't care what Mother said, I was not going to bring up Thomas and Wesley.

"Is it possible to dream of people you have never met, Dr. Devereau?" I asked.

"Absolutely," she said. "Many of us go through our daily routine and we see people all day long that we really don't remember. Sometimes our minds have a tendency to recall them, especially if there is something about them that it focused on."

"But do you think our minds can make up people we have never seen?"

"On a subconscious level, our minds can play a lot of tricks on us, Amanda."

Dr. Devereau looked at her clock on the wall. "I have another client coming in a few minutes. By the way, if you're interested in your I.Q score, let me know and we can test you on the next visit."

I wanted to know. I had to see her again.

Dr. Devereau kept me intrigued during the second session talking about fashion and glamor, but I became bored with her lack of organizational skills. At the third session

Dr. Devereau determined my intellect was ab

for a sixteen-year-old, something I already knew. Du

the next part of the session, Dr. Devereau sat me in a kid's

playroom and asked me to place square pegs in square holes

and round pegs in round holes on the board. *What's this*

about? I thought. I didn't like it; it seemed patronizing, to

treat me like I was a child. She was intentionally provoking

me. I could see it in her eyes.

"I know what you're trying to do, Dr. Devereau," I said.

She stared at her desk as if to mentally inventory her files,

ignoring me like I was invisible.

I continued playing with the pegs, placing the square

ones on top of each other and the round ones on the table

in the shape of a T.

"Are you frustrated because you can't break me?" I asked.

"You've been testing me, Dr. Devereau, and while you've been

learning about me, I've been learning about you. What you

know is what I let you know."

Dr. Devereau continued to act as though she didn't

hear me.

"I've been controlling the sessions, not you," I said.

"You're not as good as I thought you were. Do you even have

a diagnosis?" I asked.

"I do," she responded in a condescending voice. "First of

all, Amanda, I like you. You're fully aware of yourself and I

think you generally want to do the right thing. It's a struggle

that will be with you forever. With daily practice you can be ou can be successful."

evereau? What other information have

escribe me? Tell me what you think you

with a smirk.

s is our last visit, Amanda, here goes. Buckle

up,   d.

"Each morning when you wake up, you get excited with the thought of ruining someone's life. You like to play with people's feelings and watch them squirm. When you leave your house in the morning, your first thought when you cross the threshold is to not step on the square blue tiles you referred to and you don't know why. If you go to the city bus stop and you see someone get on wearing red, you wait for the next bus. The sight of one lone shoe on a sidewalk, or on the road, scares you. It's difficult for you to process why one shoe is without the other because they are a pair. You will avoid the area surrounding the shoe until it's gone. You have this and other rituals you follow every day, because if you don't, you become confused. They help to keep you grounded."

"Do you want me to go on, Amanda?" she asked with a serious tone.

"Please," I said, interested.

"You avoid eye contact with people you can't read. You don't understand why your ability to figure out people doesn't work on everyone and it frustrates you. There is goodness in you, but it conflicts with another part you can't control. As for me, I make you restless. Your signs are not uncommon Amanda."

"Now it's your turn. I want you to show me how good you are at knowing yourself, how much you think you have hidden from me."

A challenge, sure, why not, I will win. Aside from her beautiful office and excellent fashion sense, I was happy to point out to Dr. Devereau her incompetence.

"When I see a person who is emotional, Dr. Devereau, I turn away. When I see someone who is weak, I want to tear off their flesh, starting with their eyes. I don't know why. If I saw you holding on to a ledge, I might step on your hands to watch you fall, and then watch as you're dying on the ground below. After you're dead, I might cry at your hospital bed or funeral, as if I was never present at your death. I might throw a ball to see if a kid will run into the street and get hit by a car. If I'm cornered, I can cry on cue and people will come to my rescue. I haven't done those things—except for the crying - but I have come close."

"Do you want to hear more, Dr. Devereau?" I asked.

"Please continue, Amanda."

"Human emotion is a weakness for people like me to manipulate. I can suck your energy as easily as I drink from a straw. I could turn your husband, your kids, and every one of your friends against you. I'm sensitive to certain sounds. When people cry, it hurts my ears. When people laugh, I want to laugh too, but I don't know what it means. When someone tells me they love me, I tell them I love them back, but I'm not sure what love is, so I fake it; I fake sincerity, love, and sympathy, and I can fake passion so well, I could win an Oscar. I can make you love me, then turn around and kill you for your money."

"I can also read your thoughts," I continued, "and detect your weaknesses. I have an enhanced sense of smell. Right now you're taking a licorice supplement to help with your digestive problems due to nervousness. You've been ovulating each time I have come here. Your heart beat faster on sixteen occasions when you thought I had caught on to your questioning. You become extremely weak when you're excited, which means to me, you're probably submissive in bed."

Dr. Devereau was cool and didn't show any emotion.

I had to push her to get a response, so I continued.

"I can see your dark side, Dr. Devereau. You try to keep it at bay, but sometimes it comes out and you do bad things. My instincts are remarkable. I consider myself to be superior to you and others like you. You are substandard, disposable. I do not react; I process. I'm sixteen and more intellectual than you are."

Dr. Devereau had tried to belittle me and I blurted everything I could think of, determined to show I was stronger than her.

She sat straight-faced in her chair, listening to every word I said.

"Amanda, you meet most of the criteria for being a sociopath, in case you hadn't figured it out."

"I already know," I replied.

"I thought you hadn't been to a psychologist. How could you possibly know this, Amanda?"

"I've had to learn how to be a person."

"You've done extraordinarily well. You're one of the lucky ones, so far."

"I practice in front of a mirror every day to learn the proper responses to human behavior just enough to fit in," I said. "Fortunately, people see what they want to see, so it hasn't been as difficult as I thought it would be."

"There's still a lot more to learn, Amanda. You need to understand that you are also vulnerable. There is a type of predator out there that can hurt you. They will find you to be a threat, and others like police and social workers can exploit your weakness in terms of not being able to feel. I can help you to recognize them for your own safety and also to control and manage your symptoms."

"I'm done, Dr. Devereau." Then I stood up and walked out to Mother.

When I looked back Dr. Devereau was signaling Mother to go in.

When Mother came out a few minutes later, she looked toward me frozen with fear; it was almost eerie.

I surmised that Mother heard five words she would never forget:

"Your daughter is a sociopath."

CHAPTER 5

AN ALTERED STATE OF MIND

I CAME CLOSE TO COMMITTING MURDER TWO TIMES IN MY life. The first was when I listened to Mother tell the story of my diagnosis to Daddy, and the second was when she told our close family members I was born with a disease.

I stood over her that first night for three hours in the dark holding her favorite Wusthof kitchen shears, ready to cut her throat while she slept. I wanted so badly to chop her into little pieces and feed her to the neighbor's dog.

Daddy told Mother he didn't think there was anything wrong with me. "You're making a big deal out of nothing," he told her. He and I are a lot alike; besides, Daddy always protected me. Mother resented Daddy for loving me more than he loved her.

Mother set the tone for how I was going to be treated by people around me. It made no difference that I had done so much work to fit in. All because of what she said, I was treated differently. I had a disease. Fortunately, it forced me to learn even more about being a sociopath; I knew everyone around me would try to learn about it, so I had to be sure I knew more.

There was no internet back then like there is now, so I spent a lot of time at the library. I researched Sociopathy and learned as much as I could. I explored every medical journal, reference book, and article I could get my hands on. I took several well-known tests used by psychologists and each confirmed I was a sociopath. I gained a deep understanding of my condition; it helped me cope with symptoms and control my sociopathic tendencies.

A survey I took in a *Journal of Modern Medicine* classified me as "functional," not a bad sociopath or one with homicidal tendencies. Mari had confirmed the same with Kathryn too.

After a few months, I accepted the permanence of my fate. I was different from everyone else and the logical decision was to not only learn to live with it, but to embrace its uniqueness and be sure I knew how to use it to my full advantage. The upside was that people like me were successful CEO's, politicians, and Wall Street executives making exorbitant salaries. The downside was I would be unable to stop this need to fill something inside me apparently. The other downside according to my research was that it was in my nature to target others and manipulate people around me for my own selfish needs. *Isn't that what people do to each other anyway?* I thought.

Mother didn't waste any time following Dr. Devereau's advice. Her plan was for me to meet Dr. Samson, a well-known clinical psychiatrist who specialized in matters dealing with mental disorders. That's what Mother called it.

Dr. Samson was well respected in the medical community with an established practice in Medford, Massachusetts just north of Boston. Mother announced that she and I were scheduled to leave early on a Monday morning for a four-thirty afternoon appointment. There was no discussion; she was on a mission, and though I didn't want to miss two days of school, I had no choice.

On the way to the airport, Mother handed me an article from *The Journal of Psychiatry*. It described Dr. Samson's work as innovative and quantitative. His bio made Dr. Devereau look like an amateur. Mother chose him for a reason, but I don't think she was prepared for what he would find when he delved into the deepest layers of my mind.

CHAPTER 6

FULL DISCLOSURE

THE SIX-HOUR PLANE RIDE, COMBINED WITH THE MASSES OF people at the airport, was exhausting. Mother drove the rental car for twenty-minutes on I-93 North and then West in the vicinity of Tufts University to Dr. Samson's office. Mother was a stickler about arriving on time, so there was no stopping. We arrived sweaty and tired to a brown single story office complex. It was a brisk 49 degrees outside. It surprised me when I stepped out, waking me from my dreary travel stupor. Mother put her arm around me as we walked toward the building with dark reflective windows. We were met at the door by Dr. Samson's assistant, Martha, who welcomed us in.

"Hi, Mrs. Preston. Hi, Amanda," Martha said firmly. "Thank you for being on time. You must be tired. The rest of the afternoon has been reserved for you. Can I get you a tonic or anything?"

Mother and I moved to sit on the sofa. "We're fine, thank you," Mother responded for the two of us.

The waiting room was furnished in style, with a worn leather couch and a matching chair, old-style metal buttons stitched in a pattern on the arms. I sat across from Mother on the chair. My mind focused on the discolored and worn spots where others had sat before. *What were their expectations, what did they learn?* I wondered. I pictured famous people sitting quietly under a veil of silence to conceal the secret I too was hiding. Mother picked up an issue of a women's magazine lying on the coffee table, opening it to a page on diets. The headline facing toward me read "How to spice up your time in bed with your partner."

The walls of the waiting room were covered with paintings of a log cabin by a stream and a field of yellow and blue flowers as far as the eye could see. The setting in the paintings seemed peaceful and inaccessible to people. My impression was that Dr. Samson might wish to retire to that environment.

After a few minutes, a stocky, light-haired balding man about 5'5" opened the door that had a plaque, "Dr. Samson, Clinical Psychiatrist." Wearing the traditional white doctor coat, he walked directly toward Mother and me. He looked slightly disheveled and had an accent, though I couldn't place it exactly. He resembled someone from that *Mad Scientist* show.

"Good afternoon, Mrs. Preston. Hi Amanda. It's a pleasure to meet you both," he said with a smile. "Please come into my office where we can talk."

I walked in behind Mother. We sat in the two seats facing Dr. Samson's. My eye caught a glimmer of perspiration above his right ear and I noticed his face was pale. His eyes looked reddish, giving me the impression he had been up most of the night before. He looked tired. For a moment, we sat quietly facing each other. I was picking up extreme stress in Dr. Samson. My instinct told me he was suffering from a serious health problem. His breathing seemed labored. *High blood pressure*, I thought.

Dr. Samson explained to Mother and me how he performed patient evaluations. He said he was primarily involved in research projects and saw only one patient per month. He took a moment to describe his method.

"I follow the medical standards of providing a diagnosis, but I have my own process for measuring a person's mental condition. It will take two hours in session to assess personality traits, conversational ability, individual strengths, relationships, and emotional capacity," he said.

"Can I request a copy of your report, Dr. Samson?" Mother asked.

"Yes, Ms. Preston, all of this will be made available to you. If it's agreeable, I would like to begin immediately. And then we can discuss treatment."

Mother stood up, walked over and hugged me. "I love you, Amanda," she said.

Dr. Samson walked Mother to the door and advised her to return at exactly six thirty to pick me up.

Mother left and the door closed behind her.

Without mincing words, Dr. Samson asked, "What do

you sense about me, Amanda? Give me your first impression."

I could see that Dr. Samson dealt with things on a matter-of-fact basis and I respected that about him. Not knowing if I would get the opportunity to speak to a man with his qualifications again, I wanted to do my best so he could see me and try to peel back the layers. Dr. Devereau wanted to diagnose me; Dr. Samson wanted to treat me.

"The truth," Dr. Samson insisted. "It's how I prefer we communicate. You will learn enough from me today to change your life, Amanda. There's no need for you to lie, use pity, or make up stories, or use any other distractions to test me. From this moment forward, I expect you to speak and respond to me with complete honesty. Can you do that for me?"

"Yes," I said. It was my chance to show Dr. Samson how smart I was. Inside, I thought back to Kathryn's sessions, and wondered if she had been honest with Sara's mom.

"Good. Start with the most basic thought then move onto the complex."

"The scent from your pores tell me you recently ate smelly cheese and garlic; you're in your late seventies, and stubborn. Based on how your colleagues describe your work in medical journals, you lack respect in the psychiatric community. You're very conservative and have probably been married to the same woman for over forty years, someone you met in college. No children. You grew up in an upper-class family, most likely as an only child. An I.Q. test would put you in the 140 range, identifying you as extremely intelligent. You have limited hearing in your left ear from the way you turn one-quarter to the right to hear, trauma you may have sustained when you were in the military. The scarring on your left hand is from serious burns and so I'm surmising from that and your age that you saw battle. You become bored easily and based on the fact that you'll see only one person per month, you're completely caught up in your research. Like most intellectuals, you're generally a loner. You're diabetic and your levels are dangerously unstable due to your bad diet. You have chosen to spend the last few years of your life working on an attempt to understand how the human brain works. You also lack emotion, the capacity to feel remorse and guilt—similar to a sociopath. You don't know how much longer you have to live, but you still work tirelessly because you believe you're close to a breakthrough."

"That's enough, Amanda," he said abruptly. "What is your date of birth?" he asked.

"My birthday is August 25, 1972, and I'm sixteen years of age."

"Do you know the difference between what is acceptable in society versus what is not?"

"I do, Doctor, and doing the right thing is important to me."

"Why?"

"Because I don't want to go to jail—"

"Let's move on," he interrupted. "How do you relate to your parents?"

"I hate Mother; she watches every move I make. She sees through my mask. Daddy loves me, though. He's the opposite of Mother."

"What mask are you referring to?"

"I hide behind a mask everyday so people don't see who I really am."

"What is wrong with who you are Amanda," he asked?

"I am not a nice person."

"And your little brother?"

"Jamie's normal—he cries and everything. He figured me out early. He is what he is."

"Do you have many dreams, Amanda?"

"I have a few."

"What about?"

"I dream of people I don't know being hurt. And sometimes I dream of two dead bodies that live in my closet."

"Dead bodies? Let's move on to another item," Dr. Samson said. "We can leave your dreams to another person I know who specializes in that subject. Next," he asked, "do you have any limitations?"

"Just to not break the law," I answered.

"Any physical limitations?" he asked.

"None really. I've accepted what I am, Dr. Samson."

"If you could choose one, tell me what it would be. Remember, the logical thing to do is to tell the truth,

Amanda," Dr. Samson responded.

"There are certain things I can't do," I said. "But mostly it's just the law that has placed restrictions on me and society. That's it. I can still make people my puppets."

"Puppets?"

"I can manipulate them and make them do what I want."

"How do you manage to accomplish making someone do what you want?"

"I am charming and I am beautiful," I said.

"Besides that, is there one particular thought or desire that stays in your mind for longer than a day?" he asked.

"I often think about sex," I answered, unbuttoning my top button so he could see my developing breasts. My mind wandered for a second into a scene where I pictured myself surrounded by young gorgeous men. I began to think of my beauty and couldn't concentrate on the session. I was fast becoming tired with Dr. Samson and his questions.

"Look at me, Amanda," he shouted, moving his face close to mine.

Taken aback, I suddenly began to feel odd with Dr. Samson. Uncomfortable and confused.

"Amanda," he said. "Look at me. Your mind is stuck in your last thought. It is obsessing you and not letting you break out of it."

I started to perspire and feel ill. My mind began its primal defense, setting in motion a series of countermoves to confront him, and I couldn't stop.

"Would it be okay if we were to take a break so I can get a drink?" I asked.

"Look at me, Amanda," he said softly. "You're not in danger, we are in my office and I'm asking questions to help you."

Suddenly, I shut down; I was unable to continue. I felt as if I had run a marathon and needed to stop and rest. For the moment, Dr. Samson had disarmed me.

"What is your mind obsessing about?" he asked pausing, "I'm asking you a question, Amanda." Dr. Samson could see right through my defense; he was not letting me off; I couldn't distract him. "Tell me," he insisted.

I blurted, my voice loud, "my beauty, my system, isn't complete until I can cry real tears, when I need and want to, Dr. Samson."

"What for?" he asked.

"They're pretty and Sara has them."

"What is your response when you see people cry tears Amanda?" he asked.

"I want to hurt them."

I felt weak and confused. Dr. Samson had unlocked a door in my mind and my mental shield was down.

"What is it? Tell me, I want to know Amanda, what is happening in your mind? Do people seem weaker to you if they cry; what about when they see you cry? Do you want to hurt them either way?"

"I target people to get what I want, and usually they end

up getting hurt."

"How?"

"I control them but they don't know it."

"How do you manage to control them?"

"I gain their trust; tell them what they want to hear. I'm smart; I can manipulate almost anyone I meet. And I'm pretty, and I have this beautiful body men want."

Dr. Samson looked exhausted as we both hesitated for a quiet moment.

"What type of high school relationships have you developed?" Dr. Samson asked, changing the subject.

"I have a friend. Her name is Sara."

"Tell me about Sara."

"She's sixteen, the same age as me. I've known her since I was fourteen. I refer to her as a friend because she really loves me—"

"But you don't love her?"

"No. I keep her around because as long as I have someone like her, people think I'm like them: normal. She's figured out that I'm not capable of emotion. She keeps my secret, and I trust her. Besides, she manages to keep the emotional people away from me."

"What's wrong with emotional people, is it the tears again?" he asked.

"Their emotions make them vulnerable and I get tempted to use and manipulate them."

"Are they your targets?" he asked.

"Everyone is a target" I shrugged.

"How many people do you think you have made a target, Amanda?" he asked.

"A few, I don't recall," I said.

"Did the outcome meet your expectations with each of these targets?"

"I have a 100 percent success rate. You'd have been impressed," I said.

"Before we go into the clinical questionnaire, I have one more thing to ask, Amanda. Have you ever killed anyone?"

"I've come close. But in answer to your question: No, Dr. Samson. I've never killed anyone."

Dr. Samson exhaled loudly, indicating that part of the session was over. He handed me a glass of water. "Let's move on to the clinical questionnaire now," he said. "This is my Antisocial Personality Disorder test."

An hour later the session concluded. Dr. Samson and I walked out into the waiting room, and there was Mother already. When she saw me walk in with Dr. Samson, her eyes watered as if to say, *I love you no matter what happens.* I couldn't blame her for trying to figure out what I was capable of; after all, we lived in the same house, and with all of the stories about kids killing their parents, I thought, *she can't be too cautious.*

Dr. Samson sat across from us with a serious look on his face that worried me.

Mother placed her hand on my right leg, dreading the

news Dr. Samson would surely reveal to her.

"First of all, let me start by saying there are variations of the condition Amanda has displayed. Amanda has a form of psychopathy. It's considered the least serious in terms of severity; however, it does have considerable symptoms. It can manifest by causing the person to become hyper aware and hyper paranoid, sometimes creating a permanent defensive posture. Or it can develop into an exaggerated sense of imagination of a situation or person. But it will always have a specific focus. There is a tendency for persons with this condition to work tirelessly to fulfill whatever desire it wants to possess. Symptoms usually include forms of lying, deceit and manipulation, without any remorse. The patient may incorporate crying to solicit pity, and in many cases, sex can become a tool for various benefits."

"The good news is that Amanda possesses a significant and important factor. She knows the difference between right and wrong. I would attribute this to training herself to recognize critical behavior. For example, if she physically hurts another human being or breaks the law, she will go to jail and Amanda doesn't want to place herself in that type of a situation."

"Like most others with this condition, Amanda will continue to have issues related to her understanding people's emotions and expectations. Even though she has equipped herself with tools to learn how to act, no one can predict how one person may react to a given situation versus another. She and most others can design the basic response, like providing comfort when someone is crying or angry."

"Her intuitive ability to read a person in seconds to the point of noticing enhanced neurological activity and changes in a person's physical functions can also be a great help, but only if they are used for recognizing how she should react rather than to advance her own desires. Some who have this ability also have reported having visions of others' thoughts similar to a form of telepathy. This is a powerful skill but difficult to predict how this dynamic will play out."

"Amanda, most likely will become impatient and easily bored, but her greatest strength is her strong intellectual ability. This will help to alleviate part of the void she may struggle to fill during the course of her life, as she is unable to connect meaningfully to others."

"I need to point out one very serious concern with patients who have this condition. Some have described having experienced confusion when faced with confrontation or if they are trapped. I have come to call it a trigger situation, because it triggers a strong and uncontrolled defense. When faced with helplessness, the individual may temporarily be unable to focus or speak, and sometimes will shut down and escape into their mind, obsessing about some thought. It's similar to the fight-or-flight response built into the human psyche, and in Amanda's case it seems to be mental flight instead of fight, for now, which is good. Amanda has worked very hard to be cool, calm and in control; but in these rare moments her flight will take her inward to different places. It's a shock to the system. Without it, Amanda and others like her could become psychotic. I confirmed during the session, she does have a trigger."

"Other parts of this condition can be very dangerous as well, but as I mentioned, Amanda really seems to understand what doing the right thing means. I'm going to provide you with a list of doctors who are closer to where you live and who will be able to guide you and Amanda through any future problems as they arise. Amanda mentioned she is having dreams. I'm referring her to a Dr. Bailey who is a psychotherapist; her name is on the list. Please contact her soon. She is very competent."

Mother seemed reassured listening to Dr. Samson. Her shoulders raised as though validating her own feelings about me. On the way back to the hotel Mother said she was relieved to hear Dr. Samson say I could live a normal life. I figured as long as I didn't break the law or hurt anyone, now Mother would leave me alone. She would understand me, and feel pity for me in her own way, and that would keep her off my back.

Still she monitored me seemingly around the clock. On those nights when I wasn't in my deep dreaming state, I'd go back to her bedside with those big strong scissors, stare down at her and shake my head. She never knew how close I came…

CHAPTER 7

DREAMS OF A SOCIOPATH

DR. BAILEY REMINDED ME OF A WOMAN I ONCE SAW ON television. The woman was being arrested for trying to stop a company from cutting down trees; a wacky environmentalist, definitely a throwback from the sixties. Maybe it was her flowery fashion style combined with the outdated scent of patchouli oil. It was hippie fashion. My guess is she had a mound of hair under her arms that could start a forest fire.

The books in her office had a thick layer of dust on them, and the chairs were threadbare; it looked like she was hurting for money. *Business for psychologists specializing in dream interpretation must be slim pickings*, I thought to myself.

"Amanda, how do you know when a dream is just a dream and not real?" Dr. Bailey asked.

"It's when you wake up and nothing from the dream interacts with your real life," I replied.

"Have you had a dream before where you had a vision of a person or thing, and then the next day it came true?"

"Do you mean being able to predict the future or do you mean making up people in a dream and then finding out they are real?"

"Both Amanda," she said.

"So you want to know about the people that walk through my mind at night? People reveal themselves in dreams Dr. Bailey. You have to look at them real close because they try to hide."

"Why do they hide, Amanda?"

"Because they're up to something. They want to control you. But they cannot control me like they did Kathryn," I said.

"Who is Kathryn?"

"Kathryn was a patient of Sara's mom. She was a socio-path who couldn't control herself, couldn't say no, and was used by a bunch of men. She got pretty messed up. I dream of men too. But they won't control me. I take care of them right away; then they're gone from my dreams."

"Like who, Amanda? Who has been in your dreams, and how do you take care of them?"

"You know," I replied.

"I'm not entirely sure," she said.

"Like when I was twelve, I dreamed that Kevin at my school said bad things about me. When I woke up, I remem-bered what he said in my dream, so I stopped him before he could spread rumors and lies about me."

"You stopped him, how?"

"I told him there was a guy at school with a knife who wanted to kill him. I told him he would get all bloody and his heart would be eaten by wild animals."

"That's scary. Did you think of that all by yourself, Amanda?"

"Daddy said if I told that to Kevin, he would leave me alone."

"What happened after you told him, Amanda?"

"He just ran away from me crying. Then something bad must have happened to him. I heard Mother say he went missing. It was in the news and everything. The police searched the whole town but never found him."

"Did you do something to him, Amanda?"

"No, but I dreamed about him after he disappeared."

"What kind of dream?"

"He would stand in the middle of my room dressed in the red and black flannel shirt he was wearing when he disappeared and stare at me. He kept trying to tell me something but I couldn't understand him. He would come to me every night. Then all of a sudden he stopped."

"Then this pretty lady with long black hair started coming. I would dream of her every night and I could see her face. She was terrified and scratching like she was being hurt. Then she stopped just like Kevin."

"What is happening now? Is there another dream? Why has your mom made the appointment for you to see me?"

"I have a recurring dream Dr. Bailey, that's why I'm here. It won't go away. It gets me really tired and it's interfering with school. I've had this dream off and on since I was fourteen, but now they're coming every night and their watching me all the time. Mother said if I didn't agree to talk to you about it, she would send me to boarding school."

"Does your mother know what your dream is about?" she asked.

"No, I don't tell her stuff because she hates me. She won't let me out of her sight."

"Tell me about your dream, Amanda. Tell me who is watching you, and I'll try to help you through your problem."

I didn't have my guard up. Dr. Bailey was genuinely concerned about helping me. She fit the profile of the helper. *A pot-smoking hippie like Dr. Bailey might have an interesting perspective*, I thought.

"I have these bodies that stay with me in my room every night."

"Where do they stay? Why do you have them?"

"They stay in the closet, on the right side hidden behind my clothes."

"You keep them behind your clothes." Dr. Bailey responded surprised.

"How many are there, Amanda?"

"Two. I keep them in the closet and I take them out every night after I go to bed."

"You do?" she asked nervously.

"Why do you take them out? Do you play with them?"

"I have to take them out or they get mad. One is a woman and the other is a man. I don't know who they are or where they came from. They just showed up one night."

Alarmed, Dr. Bailey questioned, "What kind of bodies are we talking about, Amanda? Dead, alive, or what?"

"They're human but they're not completely dead; they have a strong presence. I try to keep them apart because they don't seem to really like each other."

"Where are they now?"

"I don't know. Where I left them? I don't know what they do during the day; I only see them at night."

"Are they people's bodies, Amanda? I'm not clear."

"Bodies, people bodies, you know, like us, with skin," I insisted.

"Who are these bodies?"

"Neither of them have faces, so they aren't anyone in particular. I keep them in my room in a closet so no one else will find them."

"What happened to the faces?" she asked in a panic-stricken voice.

"I don't know, but as I get older, I think I'm supposed to see their faces, just like Kathryn did."

"Oh, okay," Dr. Bailey said, as she leaned back in her chair. "Tell me how these bodies fit into your dream. What do you do with them? Are they your friends?"

"I don't think they are; it just seems like we were thrown together, and we're supposed to do this thing we do. I don't have an explanation for it."

"Please go on."

"It always starts the same. I'm lying down on my bed; I look toward the closet, at the two wooden doors. I'm tired, but I have to bring them out. First I take the man's body and lay it on my bed. I unwrap him. I only see him from his chest down to the top of his ankles. I don't see his head or feet but I know they are there; the dream is kind of clouded, so I never see his face. He's just like a real man. When I touch him, he has real skin, but he doesn't seem to be heavy for me to move."

"How are they wrapped?"

"In plastic and it's really tight."

"Do the bodies have a pulse? Are they breathing?"

"I don't think they have bodily functions, I replied.

"What purpose do they serve if they aren't supposed to be living?"

"To serve me, Doctor. I'm the one who takes care of them, and protects them."

Dr. Bailey nodded. "What happens next Amanda?"

"I sit the man on the living room couch so his penis is close to me and is within my reach. I sit on my beige footstool and I start touching it and licking the top of it. It doesn't get excited, so I just work on it over and over."

"Where is the other body, the woman? What is her body doing?"

"She is still lying on the counter a few feet away, still wrapped—I haven't unwrapped her yet."

"Why don't you unwrap her? What is she doing?"

"She's watching me suck and play with the man's penis. She doesn't know that I know she is watching me. I want her to watch me; there's nothing she can do about it."

"How is she watching?"

"Her eyes are turned toward me."

"Is she getting angry?" asked Dr. Bailey.

"She is wondering why I haven't unwrapped her; she's still in the plastic and can't move."

"Does she know the man?"

"I'm not sure. She doesn't say anything, she just stares as she's lying on the counter within a few feet, and I'm right in her view."

"Who is the woman? Can you try and picture her face? Do you know who she is?"

"I don't know, Doctor. I told you, their faces are blurred, I can't see them."

"What is the purpose of you touching the man? Does he excite you?"

"I'm not sure."

"Are you trying to have sex with him?"

"It's more like I just want him to want to have sex. I don't know if I necessarily want to have sex but he won't get excited and I don't know why. I am ready but he can't do it."

"Have you tried talking to him, Amanda? Have you asked him what you can do, or asked him if something is wrong?"

"How can I do that, Doctor? I don't even know who he is. What if he's dead, he doesn't have a face; Are you listening to what I'm telling you?"

"What do you do after you realize the body won't or can't have sex with you?" Dr. Bailey asked, ignoring my question.

"I glance over at the woman and I think of her begging me to love her."

"Have you ever approached her, Amanda?"

"When I get bored playing with the man's penis, I start to walk over to her. I tremble at the thought of getting close to her."

"Do you ever unwrap her Amanda?"

"She might have a face and maybe I don't want to know who she is, so I don't."

Dr. Bailey's hand reached for her glass of water, appearing troubled. "Can you take a closer look at her?" she asked.

"If I get within a foot or so of her, I see the outline of her finger start to move under the plastic. When I stop moving toward her, she stops. If I take another step, the plastic over her nose starts to swell as if she's breathing. She's not supposed to. Neither one of them is supposed to breathe."

"Does the image of this woman frighten you? You don't seem to frighten easily."

"I don't know," I said.

"Have you ever tried unwrapping the woman first?"

"I can't, Dr. Bailey. I have to unwrap the man first, that's how it plays out; I can't change the order of things." I sighed.

"Now they're starting to come to me during school, using their thoughts to try and get me to come home and take them out during the day."

From the look on Dr. Bailey's face, she was deeply concerned about my dream.

"I want you to do something different tonight, Amanda. I want you to still take them out, but I want you to try and unwrap the woman and look at her. Don't be afraid; she can't hurt you. I believe that after you see her, you will stop having the dreams. Focus on the woman instead of the man."

"I'll try, Dr. Bailey, but can you tell me what the dream means?"

"The best I can do, Amanda, is give you an idea; but I think what I told you will work. The dream has different meanings and each item in the dream has significance. From the information you continue to emphasize, my guess is that by being with the man, you are experiencing the ultimate form of control over him. You are also controlling the woman by placing her on the counter where she can watch. You could also be experimenting with sexuality."

Dr. Bailey and I took a break after the session and shared a pastry. She let me pet her retriever, Taboo.

Mother arrived within minutes. She was wearing her successful businesswoman power suit with her favorite red blouse.

"Come in and sit down, Mrs. Preston," Dr. Bailey said.

Mother sat next to me. She had become tired and weary of doctors and the different opinions they offered. To her, this was no different. She remained silent and expressionless.

"Mrs. Preston, I've listened to Amanda's dream over the past hour and there isn't anything I would be concerned about. The information of the dream she discussed is confidential; however, I believe she is experiencing puberty and is curious about the male body and psyche. It's a normal response for a girl her age. In conclusion, Mrs. Preston, I found Amanda to be very open and, more importantly, honest about her experiences. I trust her completely."

I went to bed that night and stared at my closet doors. This time, the urge to take them out wasn't so strong. Maybe the idea of unwrapping the woman scared the man too, because they weren't pulling me so much anymore; but I knew they were still watching me.

CHAPTER 8

DADDY'S FRIEND

THE DIAGNOSIS FROM DR. BAILEY EMPOWERED ME BUT IT also made me restless. In some ways I began feeling claustrophobic inside and needed to stretch my wings…

Each Friday afternoon, Sara would be picked up by her mother and taken to piano lessons somewhere in the valley. She usually didn't get back until six-thirty, so I'd hurry home and run straight up to my room to concentrate on my homework.

It was automatic for me to look across the road toward Sara's room window and wave when I reached the second-story landing. We timed it perfectly. This particular Friday, however, I was surprised to see her dad vacuuming the upstairs' carpets.

I liked Mr. Rousseau; he and Mrs. Rousseau made an attractive couple. They always made breakfast for Sara and me on Saturday mornings when I stayed at their house. Sara said her father was super intelligent and a CEO of some telecommunications company. He always helped out around the house and had become a good friend of Daddy's. A supreme dresser too, and nice-looking enough for forty-five, although he was someone I had a difficult time figuring out. He sometimes got nervous around me, but he would always stay polite and cordial.

This time when I saw him, I waved out the window to Mr. Rousseau across the way. He saw me, smiled and waved back.

Neatly placing my schoolbooks on my round chair, I faced the mirror to remove my sparkly hair ties. My thoughts wandered, from the math homework to how handsome Mr. Rousseau was for his age. Still disappointed from my experience with Thomas, I needed stimulation, and Mr. Rousseau appeared available. But first I needed to know his weakness. So I came up with a plan.

Still directly in Mr. Rousseau's line of sight, I continued to face the mirror with my back toward him so he could see my shapely bottom in tight jeans. Using an example of a girl in a movie I had seen, I swayed my hips, as if I was dancing to music, bending over to brush my long blonde hair, and then throwing it back. But Mr. Rousseau hadn't noticed me. In the mirror, I could see him moving around in Sara's room, vacuuming.

Just as I began to turn and walk toward my desk, resigned to do homework, from the corner of my eye I saw him pause and look in my direction. Quickly, but smoothly I stopped and resumed my performance. I deliberately began to pull my sweater upward moving my hair side to side as I got it off. I rubbed some lotion on my stomach and on my lower back knowing he could see. The mirror allowed me to catch his quick reaction. I could see his facial expression change, even from where I was—he looked eager and hungry, and slightly embarrassed; but I didn't care. The feeling of control stirred me inside and I became aroused by Mr. Rousseau.

It just so happened I was wearing my favorite pink bra. Mr. Rousseau would surely notice because it complemented my medium-sized breasts. They were much more developed than most sixteen year olds. Hoping he was still focused on me, I slowly removed my bra; first the right strap, allowing it to fall over my arm, then the left, as I unclipped the back and let it fall to the floor. In the mirror Mr. Rousseau was at full attention mesmerized at how beautiful I am. He had no idea I was watching him watch me. At that moment, without his knowing, I knew his weakness and he was completely exposed to me.

I unbuttoned the top button of my jeans and pulled the zipper downward, working my hips from side to side in an effort to wiggle them off. By this time, Mr. Rousseau was getting a glimpse of my pink panties as I pulled my jeans two inches further down exposing the two dimples on my lower back. The rush of being watched boosted my sense of power to a point so much more than Thomas could ever have done. My blood began to feel hot, coursing through me.

But I wasn't finished. I needed to go further and keep this thrill going.

I slipped out of my jeans letting them fall to below the

back of my knees. I twisted my upper body and exposed my breasts to Mr. Rousseau in full view. I quickly turned back toward my mirror to watch the flutter on his face. When my eyes focused on the spot in the mirror where I could see him behind me, he was gone. But I was sure he had seen everything.

I wanted more control. I was ready and I was sure he was too, but I couldn't just drop over and throw myself on him. I wanted to do it but I needed to be smarter than him. I wanted to give him my virginity. But first, he had to earn it. He would worship me. Besides, I was bored. I couldn't let anyone see or find out especially my parents. It would be an excuse for Mother to send me away.

After a few minutes, I put on shorts and a tight t-shirt, and laid out my math homework to keep up appearances. I decided to go bra-less. My mind was made up; I didn't care if it was wrong morally. It wasn't wrong legally. With a sense of excitement in my body, I hurried over to Sara's house.

I'm not sure why, but I knocked this time instead of using the doorbell. Something told me the bell would affect me, (they had before, but I couldn't understand why). Mr. Rousseau opened the door. He looked surprised to see me. I paused. I couldn't help but to stare at his gorgeous facial features, high cheekbones and green eyes. The sight of his shiny black hair combed straight back, wearing his Brioni suit pants and button down shirt almost made my heart skip a beat.

"Hi Amanda, I'm sorry, I have to run. Sara's not here. She's at piano. I was just heading out to a meeting," he said.

I could tell that he was nervous because he stood close to the door with his right hand clenched to the doorknob. But he wasn't giving me any real signal that he was in a hurry, or that he wouldn't let me in.

"Mr. Rousseau, can I get a book from Sara's room?" I asked. "I talked to her earlier and she had said it would be fine. I need it for my homework, and I know she won't be home for an hour."

His eyes fixated on my face, trying not to stare at my erect nipples. I could feel his pulse racing, and him struggling to maintain control.

"Of course, Amanda, go on up and get it. I'll wait right here for you."

I ran up the stairs, knowing that my loose shorts revealed the pink panties he saw me wearing earlier. At the top of the stairs, I stopped for a moment to flip my hair back just enough to see his expression as he watched my every move.

In Sara's room, I grabbed the first book I saw on her table, which happened to be a calculus binder. Walking quickly down the stairs, I saw Mr. Rousseau still standing in the spot where I had left him.

"I found it," I yelled out cheerfully.

I walked slowly down the steps looking towards him only to see he still hadn't taken his eyes off of me. He was absorbed by me. The green of his eyes seemed shiny and glazed. His look was fiery and the bulge in his pants had become noticeable. I knew he wouldn't be able to resist.

When I got to the bottom, I stopped for a second to face him. Then I moved closer and placed my right hand in his left palm; instead of pulling away, he squeezed it enough that I could feel his heartbeat. He smelled sweet and his upper lip had a trace of perspiration.

Mr. Rousseau stepped around me to hold the front door open. I turned quickly to hug him with both arms, and before he had a chance to react, I put my lips onto his. Surprised, he pulled away as if he had been burned by a hot object. My power was fierce and I could see the look in his eyes was like Thomas's, except a hundred times more intense. He was weakening, unable to fight beginning to succumb to me. I pushed the door shut and placed his hand on the warmth between my legs. Pulling up my shirt, I exposed my breasts, and began rubbing my pubic area against his, feeling his erection growing harder. Then I unzipped his pants and took out his penis and began caressing the tip until a small glimmer of fluid rested on top. He caught his breath and I heard a small moan escape his mouth. Still unsure, he placed his head on my chest and both his hands around my waist and eased us both down to the floor.

"I can't do this, Amanda," he said. "You're an attractive young woman, but I just can't hurt my family. What is happening to me," he sobbed.

"No one will know," I whispered. "You can trust me not

to tell anyone. I know you want me.

Earlier, my mind had already predicted the outcome for Mr. Rousseau. There was no possibility of changing it. I knew that if I wanted him, I'd have him, and he'd have no choice in the matter. That's how it works with me. I get whatever and whoever I want. I had come for him, so he was mine.

I leaned over him and moved my body on top. I took out a condom from my shorts pocket that I got from Mother's nightstand. I tore the right corner and rolled it out, slowly placing it on his member. He remained breathless staring at my beauty. "Don't worry, it'll be our secret."

I took his erection in my hand and placed it between my thighs. The throbbing he was experiencing seemed primal to me. Mr. Rousseau was an intellectual man but at this moment he could just as well have been an extinct cave dweller. *I have this power over him just by having this body*, I thought. It was an undeniable fact, exhilarating beyond my previous imagination. His hands moved slowly under the back of my shirt, pushing my top upward while he caressed the curves of my back. Then his hands slid forward until he reached my breasts. I felt the pressure of his penis against my belly as he began to push. Then he pulled my mouth to his and stuck his tongue deep inside. He continued to kiss and taste me, my face, ears, chest, nipples. I could smell the intensity of his mating scent; he was taking control and I couldn't have stopped him even if I had wanted to.

He turned me over and laid me down onto Mrs. Rousseau's exquisite eighteenth century Persian rug in the foyer. I stared at the ceiling as Mr. Rousseau deftly pulled off my shorts with his long arms. By this time, he had completely lowered his pants and I could see his large erection. Surprised, I stared to see the condom I placed earlier appear fully extended and I became frightened. But it was too late.

I was unable to move, trapped by his hands clasped on mine, above my head. He had become more aggressive, his sexual predatory instincts heightened, and I felt his body swell as he lay on top of me.

I couldn't reach to completely remove my panties; his penis rubbed eagerly against me, pushing them aside, moving inward through my pubic hair, working its way to penetrate inside. I felt an intense shock of pain come over me.

My body began shaking. I felt him inside. His weight seemed staggering as he continued pushing deeper and deeper. His muscular force was overwhelming. The pain of his penis pushing into me became unbearable. His kissing smothered my screams momentarily while I struggled to catch my breath. I couldn't speak. I lay on the floor. He continued to thrust again and again, moving me across the Persian rug until my head hit the hardwood floor. After a few more minutes of thrusting, he let out a whimper, then I felt him release. As my body lay limp and helpless, I turned to face Mr. Rousseau.

His penis slid out of me and he sat back to catch his breath. His brow was wet and he looked exhausted. He reached down to remove the condom that appeared torn and lightly stained with blood—my blood. He hurried to put his pants on.

"What have I done," he mumbled using his sleeve to wipe the sweat from his forehead.

My body was slow to move; my arms felt wobbly and my hips seemed heavy.

Mr. Rousseau grabbed my right arm and helped me up. He wanted me to go. I quickly put on my shorts and shirt.

"Thank you, Mr. Rousseau," I said quietly. "I better get home."

When I opened the front door to leave, the fresh air helped me regain my composure. At home I quickly drew a bath to clean off the sticky semen and blood on my inner thighs. Weakened from the experience, I sat in the bath to let the warm water soothe me.

Later in the evening, I watched Sara and her mom arrive from piano practice. Sara waved to me as usual.

Mr. Rousseau canceled poker because Daddy didn't go over that Friday night and there were no lights on when I looked toward their house. It appeared they had left for the weekend.

On Monday of the following week, I heard from Sara that something happened to her father. She didn't give details. It was the last conversation we had. They suddenly moved away and I never saw Sara or Mr. and Mrs. Rousseau again.

CHAPTER 9

SOCIOPATHIC INTELLECT

I HEARD AN ARGUMENT BETWEEN MOTHER AND DADDY. IT involved my sexual experience with Mr. Rousseau. *He couldn't keep his mouth shut could he? That's a real problem with empaths; they have such a hard time keeping a secret. Sara's Dad was just like her.*

The heated discussion made Daddy upset, and for days he wouldn't speak to me or Mother over what happened. Mother got her way and decided once and for all I was evil. She somehow arranged for me to graduate high school a year early, and, at seventeen, I found myself scheduled to begin the fall semester at the University of California. Early on a Friday, Mother threw the few bags of clothes I had packed into the car, and drove us all the way to Berkeley, stopping only once for gas and a quick bite in Medford. There wasn't a lot of talking. She was relieved to be rid of me. I thought it was odd Daddy never came to see me off.

The campus looked huge, surrounded by long rows of lofty trees, plush green grass, and a large soccer field where an event was taking place. One side of the campus was office-like and the other looked like a long row of Swiss chalets. Due to my late enrollment (actually I'll bet it was because of strings Mother pulled), I was placed in a single room at the all-female dorm in the office-like portion, closer to the recreation and workout areas.

We found our way to Stern Hall and room 425. Again, I found myself surprised. Mother spared no expense. Though we were exhausted from the drive, we unloaded everything within an hour or so. We went to dinner at some ethnic place along University Ave, and then checked into the Hotel Durant for a night. The next morning was spent at a local Crate & Barrel for odds and ends.

During the day, I noticed moments when Mother's eyes would water as if she was holding back her emotions. The most notable was when we made the bed up just like my room in Happy Valley. "Pull down the corners like this Amanda," she said, stretching the sheets. I wasn't able to completely understand—I know she didn't like me—but I guess she was still sad somehow knowing her only daughter was gone. For my part, I was beginning to accept my fate. She had surprised me but this move was unlike her. It didn't make sense. It just gave me freedom and a lot more chance and opportunity to pursue whatever I wanted.

Mother and I went out for what seemed like our final lunch. It was quick since she needed to get back on the road for the long drive home. When I turned to look at her to say goodbye she began to weep; even that was unfamiliar, not like the time I told her about Thomas. This cry had a sense of defeat, of being broken.

"Please understand I love you Amanda, and no matter what happens, you will always be my little girl. I will love you forever. I'll only be a phone call away," she said as she turned away. When she was facing away, mother let out a cry. "May you and God forgive me one day," she said looking up towards the sky.

"I know, Mother," I said, "I can always count on you. I'll be fine." At that, I rushed back to my room to finish organizing my things.

Time moved quickly; busy with school, I never made time to call home. I got jobs in the summer, so I couldn't go back to Happy Valley to visit. I talked to Daddy a couple times, but I never spoke with Mother at all, in the entire four years, which was all right with me. She never tried to call me either, so it must have been okay with her too.

I'm sure they were glad, relieved I was gone.

The stipend from Mother was more than enough to pay for what I needed. The extra money they sent me to come home for break and holidays was well spent on the latest fashions from the likes of Gucci or Dolce & Gabbana. I had no interest in going home anyway; why would I? Even Daddy didn't push for me to visit; by the time I was twenty-one they had to have realized that I was never going home.

One thing for sure is that Dr. Bailey's lessons on how to control my dreams helped a lot. I would still dream of those two bodies in my closet but the more I attempted to go towards the woman to unwrap her like Dr. Bailey said, the dream would suddenly end. I never did manage to unwrap her. Other dreams had subsided too except for another strange one where I would see people's faces as I was hurting and killing them.

Dr. Samson however, was full of shit. Yes, in high school I had done very well in classes, and he told me I had a high intellect. But in fact what I really had was a shrewd and cunning sense about people, not quite the same thing as intellect. My years in college opened up some deficiencies and competency issues to my shock and dismay. I had no choice but to acknowledge and accept the reality that I did not possess the abilities to become a CEO or CFO simply based on my smarts as I had earlier believed. My education and experiences taught me that I don't have the mental aptitude, even though I had high goals and capacities in other areas. I knew that in my case intellect was not the determining factor of my future. I had something better. I had the ability to read people, to influence their thoughts and behavior. And, not having to think about emotional garbage allowed me ample time to concentrate on my own goals.

I switched my interests from academics to the people around me that I could convince to help me. You should have seen me, I created a different façade for each person I needed in my life. Liz, who considered me like a sister, did most of my papers and exams. I liked to play a game with her.

One day I would be nice. Then on another day, I would be mean and refuse to talk to her. It drove her crazy. She would become a wreck. The more I abused her, the more she wanted to be with me. I thought it was amusing.

And Tim—I needed him because he was a math genius. He suffered from low self-esteem, probably because students would tease him for his flamboyant mannerisms. So I would build him up. Be there for him, talk him through, and on occasion tell him I loved him.

My dorm also happened to be close to the science building, so after a few visits to a nearby coffee shop, I met Gary. He was a total genius in engineering and chemistry. He was also nice and good looking, but had a girlfriend on campus. I got to know her so I could learn about Gary. She told me all about him, and the next day I went out and bought him a Forty Niners jacket with Mother's generous credit card. He was so grateful, he offered to tutor me for free. His girlfriend tried to interfere, but I convinced her it was okay. Gary was single-minded in his goal to become a chemical engineer and work locally in a place called Silicon Valley. I hadn't even known what silicon or its valley were.

At first I was intrigued to learn about the concept of silicon, but something happened to me during my many conversations with Gary. "It's relatively inert and less reactive than other elements, like carbon," he said. I had never understood anything so clearly. *"That's me, that's me!" I thought to myself. "It takes a lot to make it melt or boil, and it doesn't shrink when frozen like other things. My lack of normal human warmth—my cold heart - is what makes me powerful."* I connected with Silicon and its core. I had never connected with anything my whole life. I also started to obsess about my potential in such a place. I could climb multiple ladders and manipulate powerful people. The rewards would be vast, it was my destiny. I made a vow with myself that I would return to make it my home.

I cruised along with all these people essentially doing my college work for me. My system started falling apart especially near the end of the four years, but I made it.

Luckily the time went by fast but it wasn't without some drama.

In my first semester, I was reprimanded by the school dean for starting a rumor that one of my professors was gay. Then for making up stories that I was terminally ill in order to receive passing grades from my teachers during finals. A girl from my class accused me of taking her research idea and claiming it as my own. A rumor spread that I was selfish and insane—but I didn't care; it just meant I would be left alone which is what I wanted anyway.

In my last semester, I was blamed because my biology class partner, Tanya, burned her arms. Supposedly, I had given her incorrect data that caused her to mix wrong ingredients, creating a highly corrosive acid. I was interviewed by the police and had to cry because they wouldn't leave me alone. I called home, but no one called me back. When I finally had enough of their harassment, I learned about civil rights and accused the police of singling me out and creating stories to discredit me. They finally stopped.

Still, all of the drama and rumors didn't prevent guys' miserable attempts of trying to sleep with me. I could do it with any of them if I wanted. Looking back, the more valuable lessons I learned from college were not in history, math science, or literature. They were about people and men in particular. I realized that, in general, men hadn't evolved as women had. They are weak, and respond easily to visual and sexual stimulation almost exclusively. They exist primarily because of their semen, and still react to their primal instincts like animals. I was evolved, so I never lowered myself to their level; if I did, I would be as pathetic as them.

That type of behavior of course translates into behaviors bordering on the unthinkable. I was at a frat party and a drunken girl jokingly said she would put out to ten men but didn't like to use a condom. She told them they would likely contract a disease. The men lined up fast, and were high fiving. Then they started to turn against each other and physically fight for a piece of her, like animals during mating season. Some animals mate during certain times of the year and it makes them vulnerable. Every day is mating season for human men, so they are vulnerable all the time. That was a useful piece of information to me.

I received my degree in Business Law with a minor in Psychology, an ironic and appropriate conclusion to my childhood years. The concept of law came easily to me because it was based on facts without emotion. My psychology education validated the troubled relationship I had with Mother because of her obvious resentment of me.

Aside from Mother, my greatest frustration was the expectations I had placed on myself. I thought I could reach heights only dreamed about by most people, but my college years proved this different.

Still, the need for power and control grew even stronger in me. It was embedded in my psyche. I was determined to have everything I desired. I had perfected my mind and my body into tools and weapons that I could easily access to accomplish whatever I set myself to. Four years of college had merely been another laboratory for me, helping me to expand, test and refine my skills. On the last day of school, Gary brought me a large shiny silvery cone shape piece of Silicon. "It reminds me of you Amanda," he said as he handed it to me. The validation from Gary didn't matter. I already saw myself as a shiny, polished, alluring piece of silicon that could crush whatever got in its way. *I feel no kinship to people, so why not to a metalloid?* That made me smile.

CHAPTER 10

AN INTENDED CONSEQUENCE

WITH MY DEGREE I WAS ABLE TO GET A LETTER OF REFER-
ence from one of my better professors (that's another story!)
to Briscoe, a well-established law firm with a reputation
of a no-nonsense work ethic, basically a ruthless group of
attorneys who became rich from manipulating the law and
settling some of the largest cases on behalf of major corpora-
tions.

The firm was in Manhattan. When I contacted them to
discuss the job, there were no real questions, just an understanding that I had the position. I was told there was already
an apartment waiting for me that would be subsidized for the
first three months. They sent me a first-class plane ticket, and
a moving company to get my things. Although I'd promised
myself I would come back to the Bay Area, I was anxious to
get out into the world and try my skills. So just like Happy
Valley, I easily said goodbye to Berkeley and moved on.

When I arrived at JFK, the firm had a town car waiting
to take me to the apartment. It took us about a half hour to
get to just below the Lower East Side. The driver gave me

the keys when we got there, and took my suitcase up to the second floor. When I opened the door, I caught my breath. The place was fully furnished, with modern clean-lined furniture (from a hip Italian design company I discovered later). There was a bar in the living room, high ceilings and beautiful hardwood floors. I found the spotless white kitchen fully stocked, and the bathroom was to die for. On the dining table was a welcome basket of fruit with a note from the partners at Briscoe, telling me where and when to show up the following day.

I woke up the next morning actually excited to begin my first day. I had bought a red knit Alaia dress for the occasion, and wore my prized Jimmy Choo black patent peep-toe pumps. I kept my makeup fairly simple, though not exactly understated: gold eyeshadow, black eyeliner and red Dior lipstick. It was a beautiful day; even the din of taxi horns and New York City bustle added to my giddiness. I walked across the street and a block south to the Briscoe office on Fulton Street. The place was deep in the heart of the financial district; the surrounding tall buildings might have seemed imposing to some, but they just challenged me to pursue my power. (Looking back after 9/11, it is interesting to me that everything, just like everyone, has its weakness.)

I was aware that most people would think me extremely fortunate to have gotten this job, but I knew that I could get a job anywhere there were men. If a man thinks he can bang you, he will hire you. I didn't create that law of nature. I just knew how to exploit it better than anyone else I know. Men were put on this planet to wipe ass.

I walked through the big glass doors on my first day and was met by Melinda, who welcomed me to the firm. A tall, lanky, mildly attractive redhead of around forty well preserved, and dressed in expensive color-coordinated fashion, she seemed friendly enough. She didn't display cleavage, part of her serious demeanor no doubt reflecting the philosophy of the firm.

"Good morning, Ms. Preston," she said. "You can call me Melinda. I hope you are satisfied with the accommodations. The university provided us a glowing recommendation of your talents."

"Thank you, Melinda. I responded, "I'm glad to be here and very excited to be in New York, "And, please call me Amanda."

"You're very attractive Amanda" she said staring at my dark blue eyes. "I think you'll enjoy working here very much."

Melinda was one of those people I rarely came across who is difficult for me to read. Each time she said something, I found myself having to pause before I responded.

We walked through the hallways to meet the staff. It was an extremely busy workplace with no time for socializing or paying much attention to new people. Melinda seated me at a desk near a window, in a row of other cubicles with clear glass panels straight to the other end of the floor. On the desk, piled high, was a stack of claims needing research. Melinda sat with me briefly to explain the process of investigating files.

"I hope you're someone who likes to be busy, Amanda."

"I am," I said.

"I've been here for thirteen years and I think it's really an exciting place to work," she said as she reached for a file placing it on the desk in front of me.

I found out later from others that Melinda wasn't married and very private. No one really knew much about her personal life but they all liked and respected her.

"Each file will have a checklist on the inside cover like this one, identifying persons who need to be called for follow-up questions. Many reports need to be requested from investigators, police officers, doctors, contractors, etcetera," she explained. "Make a note next to each item after you have completed the task and I will review your files at the end of each day. My desk is at the other end of the aisle, so if you have any questions, please come by and ask."

After a few days, I began to receive invitations from others in the office to join them for lunch. I explained that I was much too busy and preferred to eat at my desk until I learned the job. There was a lot of activity at the firm, so it was easy to get lost in the shuffle.

Melinda would occasionally stop by on Fridays to compliment me for my thorough work on the files. At times something seemed off with her. I could detect some elevation in her heart rate and she constantly had an odor like some strong medications were reeking out from her pores.

When she leaned over to explain something to me, she would become almost imperceptibly nervous and mild perspiration usually appeared at the top of her forehead. Most of the time, she wouldn't look me straight in the eyes. *She has a difficult job*, I thought, *a lot of deadline stress in a fast-paced environment*. But it didn't seem like it should be that bad; I knew I could easily do better. That day, subconsciously, Melinda became my first target at the firm.

I began staying late, past six o'clock. Only a few people remained but they were confined to litigation, far from my area. I was surprised how much information came to Melinda's office fax machine after hours on priority issues. Each evening, I began by reading those faxes to try and understand more about how information was disseminated within the office. The more I read, the more I was surprised and disappointed that Melinda wasn't giving me more important items to work on; instead, I was limited to basic case investigation.

One Friday evening, I found a fax to Melinda indicating one of the firm's clients had received a $750,000 fine and needed the firm to file a document immediately. I saw this as a perfect opportunity and my chance to move upward in the organization. I knew she would come to the office in the morning on Saturday, so I made sure no one was around, took the document and put it in my purse. I cleared the memory on the fax machine before hurrying back to my apartment.

When I arrived Monday morning, the office was buzzing and in crisis mode. Melinda looked as though she was about to have a heart attack. I walked over and offered her my assistance. In a state of panic, she thanked me and continued searching through a stack of documents. Within an hour, word went out that Melinda wanted everyone in our section to meet in the conference room immediately.

"Good morning, everyone, I called this meeting because we are missing some very important documents. On Friday, Bulk Oil says they sent us a fax to request our assistance with a citation they received from the federal government relating to an environmental hazard at their northwest facility. Because we did not file their brief within 24 hours, the company will have to pay, and now Bulk has filed against Briscoe under our Errors and Omissions policy. I was here on Saturday morning and I didn't see any paperwork from them," Melinda told the staff. "The odd part is that my fax memory was erased. I may have misplaced the document and I need your help to find it. Please go to your offices and check all the documents you have received since Friday."

After the meeting concluded, I went back to my desk to give the appearance I was diligently looking through each file. The other employees who passed by could see how hard I was concentrating on finding this lost document. The turmoil continued throughout the day. Melinda was being yelled at by different attorneys, including Mr. Harper, one of our most senior partners. I left shortly after five.

Melinda survived the ordeal, and things went back to a

fast pace. At the end of each day, I glanced at the documents coming over her fax machine, looking for another one I could take that would get her fired. I continued to remove various pages of reports over the next several months to create doubt about her ability to manage the section. I had to give her credit because she was being yelled at almost every day by someone in top management, but she didn't crack under the stress. Melinda remained a great role model of what it meant to be a professional manager. She still came to each employee's office daily and asked if they needed anything. She was so nice; that was her weakness, because she didn't have a clue what I was doing to her or that I ever had her in my sights.

Until I could find the documents I needed to finish her off, I decided to turn up the flame. I learned of a local coffee shop she frequented, so it didn't take much effort to bump into her "accidentally". At first she was surprised to see me until I began complimenting her exquisite taste in fashion. Finally, she invited me to sit and chat while sipping coffee. Later, I offered to bring her coffee at the office, and I began to deliver a cup to her every day just the way she liked it. The more I did for her, the more she trusted me. We confided in each other about past relationships that didn't work. I even cried on her shoulder. It was by far one of my best performances. Kathryn was right—all of Melinda's defenses lowered, and she was mine. The only thing left for me to do was find a secret she might be hiding that I could exploit. It became a waiting game, until one day when she invited me to her place for a glass of wine.

The taxi took me right to Melinda's on 57th, with a great view of Central Park. I noticed a subway station half a block away that I could use to get back to my apartment later if needed. I buzzed her at the bottom.

"It's Amanda."

"Come on up," she said cheerfully.

Melinda had expensive taste. Not only were her furnishings gorgeous, but it was hard not to notice the extensive wine collection which looked at a glance like it might include some bottles of Lafite. To my surprise she took out a bottle of Veuve Clicquot La Grande Dame champagne (fitting name, I thought).

"Are we celebrating, Melinda?" I asked.

"I've been thinking about you all day," she said. "I remembered when you told me about your old boyfriend treating you so badly. You're too nice, Amanda. You do everything for them and they treat you like garbage. Maybe you should stop giving in to them so easily."

"I try, Melinda, but I'm not as tough as you are. I wish I had your strength," I replied.

Melinda complimented me at every stage, and I kept turning them back on her. At one point, we were at a draw. The whole dynamic seemed kind of odd.

"How do you manage to stay so beautiful?" I asked.

With a pause Melinda flipped her long reddish hair

upward as if in front of a camera lens for Vogue magazine.

"I like pretty things, and you're a pretty thing, Amanda."

Aha! A wave of excitement came over me, almost as tingly as when I fooled everyone about Thomas. I was thrilled by the scenario playing out in front of me. Melinda was either gay or bisexual. The missing piece I was waiting for had finally displayed itself.

I was disappointed in myself that I hadn't seen it sooner. My usual success at detecting someone's sexual preference needed some fine tuning. I had gotten it wrong with Melinda. Her interest was in *me*. I quickly shifted gears. I looked at her sitting on the couch and imagined red pubic hair between her thighs. I hadn't been with a woman before, and though she was fifteen years my senior, it didn't matter. I needed her to recommend me to take over her job when she was fired.

I stood up from my chair, champagne in hand, walked over and sat on the sofa next to Melinda. I placed my glass on the coffee table, turned to her and gently caressed her soft shiny hair. Her body was shaking. I could feel her heart pounding. I began kissing her neck and ears, slowly moving closer to her mouth. With each kiss, she began to breathe long and deep. The perspiration from her body enhanced the earthy sweet smell of her perfume. (It was Caron, I think. I had practiced and developed my senses to detect most high-end perfumes, knowing they always said something I could potentially use about the person wearing them.)

I placed my lips on hers as she moved her hand under my

blouse to feel my breasts. Then, before I could react, Melinda climbed on top of me and began moving her body, humping me like a stallion with her mare. I moved my hands up to feel under her shirt. I was amazed at the softness of her large breasts. My body became warm inside as she began rubbing the outside of my pants. I unbuttoned her jeans feeling my way around under her panties until I felt her pussy. It was warm and wet. I moved sideways so she could position herself on mine. I followed her lead, placing one of my hands on her firm, round buttocks, performing every move she did until we both reached orgasm.

It was my first orgasm. I never expected to be that intimate with her or anyone. There is something disturbingly out-of-control about it, I can't let that happen again, I thought to myself. I knew that Melinda was less in control than I was, so it was okay. From then on I knew what to expect.

Lying side by side naked on the couch, we were jolted by the loud noise of the doorbell followed by rapid knocking. Quickly dressing, Melinda went to the door and discovered a package left for her. Laughing, Melinda picked it up and carried it inside. That was my perfect excuse to get dressed and leave. We both agreed to keep our relationship secret and out of the office for fear either one of us could be terminated.

A week later, Melinda rented a car and drove us upstate to a romantic cottage resort, where she had stayed once before. We toasted to our love and engaged in wild, passionate lovemaking. It was okay with a woman, but I kind of missed the violence and complete lack of emotion that comes when I'm with a man. Melinda also seemed to expect more of a bond because we were both women. But as usual, I faked it and succeeded; Melinda gave herself to me totally and completely over the weekend.

Then, when we returned to the office, I continued on my target and remained patient.

Within days, I recognized a familiar frazzled, pale look on Melinda. Finally, the continual loss of documents began to take its toll on her. She had come to me frequently before for comfort, and I would always persuade her to remain strong. This time, she confided in me that the stress had become overwhelming and she was considering resigning to give herself time to rest. I explained that if she left, it also would be easier for us to be together. This reassured her that our relationship was real. She begged me for my support, at times saying she would die without me. I promised I would remain with her after she separated from the firm.

A week or so later, I watched Melinda walk into Mr. Harper's office. Shortly after, she stopped by to tell me her last day would be in two weeks. I congratulated her with a quick hug. We agreed to meet for a Friday night celebration.

The following Monday, I received a call from Mr. Harper to come to his office immediately. *Negotiate, negotiate*, I told myself.

"Good afternoon, Ms. Preston. I'm Mr. Harper, a senior partner here at Briscoe. Please have a seat."

"Hi, Mr. Harper. Nice to meet you, sir," I said.

"Ms. Preston, here is the situation and why I have asked you in here today. First, Melinda has given us notice that she will be leaving the firm. Secondly, she has recommended you as her replacement. Now, I understand you have been here for only a year, but she assures me that you are beyond your years in terms of maturity and your performance record here at Briscoe is excellent. She tells me that your ability to retain information is exceptional. I need you to understand that this job is demanding, and you would be expected to work long hours. I need to know if this is a position that interests you?"

"Yes, Mr. Harper, it is," I said.

"Good, then we would like to offer you the position, based mostly on Melinda's word. You would definitely be the youngest Director of Administration we have ever had at twenty-two, Ms. Preston. I see your current salary is $60,000. The pay for this position is double that amount, at $120,000, and it does come with a $20,000 discretionary allowance. This is non-negotiable. Will this offer be acceptable for you, Ms. Preston?" he asked.

"Yes, sir, I accept," I said.

CHAPTER 11

IN THE ARMS OF STRANGERS

MY LIFE BECAME A WHIRLWIND. RUNNING THE INVESTIGA-
tive division at Briscoe turned out to be the perfect job for
me, but it was much more demanding than I expected.
Managing cases from venture capital to environmental
disasters kept me busy and, more importantly, interested.
Each day was different, so there wasn't time for boredom.
I wasn't insignificant like before when I was working as an
investigator for Melinda; now I had her job.

I reported directly to Mr. Harper. He began flirting
with me within a month after taking over the division. The
promotion had of course made me much more visible, and
several men at the firm took notice of me—fresh meat—but
I had no interest in anyone that wasn't above me in rank or
wasn't useful.

I maintained my relationship with Melinda for a short
time after she left, just to be sure I was solid in her job. But
then I dumped her; she of course was devastated and threw
her emotional self at me in a pathetic attempt to keep me
around. I had to get the police involved to have her arrested

for harassment. How could she think I would stay with her? The mental breakdown she suffered after that was really of her own making.

I have to say, attorneys generally speaking were more interesting to me than other men had been in my life. They were exciting because even though they might have recognized something not quite normal about me, it didn't matter to them as long as I was making them money. Probably because they were so damn dysfunctional themselves. Anyway, I knew that there was no real use for most of them in my career and life.

The salary of my new job allowed me to start enjoying the life most people can only dream of, and that I had always known was going to be mine. All my attention to details and study of success, even as a teen, was beginning to pay off. I knew all about the finer things in life, and intended to have them all. I indulged my desire for everything luxury and representative of higher society. I found a condo on the upper east side, more befitting my status. I shopped only on Fifth Avenue—at Bergdorf Goodman and Saks mostly—and got my hair done at Bendel's.

All of this kept me occupied and satisfied—along with the long work hours—for much of the first year as Director. I loved living the big city life with all the trappings.

But I began to feel a little restless, and needed to test my people skills again. Mr. Harper had been pretty persistent with the hints, so I decided to call his bluff. He jumped at

IN THE ARMS OF STRANGERS

the chance, and made up some business trip for us to go to London together. This was good; I could get world travel out of the deal too.

So the next Friday night I was off on a flight to Heathrow. There I would be joined by Mr. Harper for a long weekend. I was twenty-three and he was seventy-one, but the age difference didn't matter to either of us. He was my means to climbing the ladder. Being that he was married, he insisted on keeping a low profile, so we arranged different flights and used assumed names. Our plan was to meet at the Savoy Hotel in room 234 at one in the afternoon. He arranged everything. It was all five stars, including me. I packed some of my finest and sexiest lingerie for a weekend of wine and sex.

My plane arrived earlier, and my taxi got me to the hotel by eleven Saturday morning. The hotel lobby and neighborhood were impressive. They let me check in early and leave my bag in the room; the concierge gave me directions and suggested I take a stroll to Covent Garden.

By the time Mr. Harper arrived promptly at one—bottle of champagne in hand—I was already arrayed on the bed in a sexy red garter, thong and heels. He stopped for a second at the threshold after swinging the door open, to gaze with a lusty smile on his face. Dropping his suit jacket to the floor, he raced over to the side of the bed. He forced his right hand under my bottom as he pulled my face to him, and we began passionately kissing, tasting each others' fluids. Slowly he moved to my thighs and began licking the outside of my panties. I finished undressing while Mr. Harper went into the bathroom to freshen up. When he walked out, I lay completely naked on the soft fine linens of the hotel bed.

"You're beautiful, Amanda. I promise you a weekend you won't soon forget," he said. I was ready to take in Mr. Harper.

He poured out two glasses of champagne; I reached for mine slowly, stretching to exhibit my large breasts.

"To our good fortune, Amanda," he said.

"And many more to come," I replied as we raised our glasses.

In my mind it was his way of saying I would soon be moving up the ladder and working with the big boys.

The taste of the champagne stimulated me all over.

"Come here, lover," I said, brushing my hair behind my ears.

Mr. Harper made his way until he was on top of me. His body was larger than I had earlier thought, but he was experienced enough so he managed to keep his weight off of me. He had a big gut, and more gray hair on his chest than on his head, but none of that mattered to me.

We began kissing until I felt him enter me. He didn't mention a condom and I figured since he was married, I didn't need protection from disease (I was already on the pill). Besides, I liked the feel of his skin rubbing up against mine.

Our lovemaking lasted twenty minutes. Mr. Harper couldn't hold himself. I didn't care. I was bedded on the finest linens and seduced with the finest champagne. At two o'clock, we dressed and headed to the Savoy Grill for steamed Cornish mussels with parsley. For the rest of that day and the next, much of our time was spent drinking champagne and engaging in hotel lovemaking. Between the sex in the bedroom, we managed to see spectacular parks and gardens, Trafalgar Square and the National Gallery. We both particularly liked the paintings by Michelangelo and Botticelli. Mr. Harper commented on his wife's lack of interest in such things, which I ignored.

On our last night, Mr. Harper informed me of a surprise waiting at the hotel. A gentleman met us in the hotel lobby. He took out a box from his silver case and removed a beautiful piece of jewelry. Mr. Harper asked me to turn while he placed around my neck a gold chain with exquisite diamond and sapphire stones. *I will soon have a promotion,* I told myself as I hugged him. As I turned to go back to the room, I realized I had dropped my manners briefly. "Thank you so much, I love it," I said with my sweet smile.

The trip with Mr. Harper made me more popular at the office. Within a month, my paycheck contained a hefty pay increase. After that, flaunting my power and appeal at the office became my obsession. Men looked at me wherever I went, and women stayed away from me. I had office snitches who would tell me who was talking about me or if I needed to watch my back. I could tell when they were lying or hiding something. They were afraid of me, and that's the way I wanted it to be. Mr. Harper would send me a message now and then, telling me to be careful about bullying my employees—but I didn't care.

Mr. Harper had obviously talked about me with other executives and it wasn't long before I was enjoying attention from them. This included Stewart, an insider near the top of the firm, who had been stopping by my office with attempts to make conversation over minor details of cases. Finally he took the plunge and told me about some important client in Paris who wanted a meeting. "It has to be in person," he said. He didn't strike me as being quite as useful to me as Mr. Harper had been, but he was good friends with my immediate bosses, so I had to be able to get something from the deal.

Stewart brought me a plane ticket the next day, looking very serious so the other employees wouldn't be suspicious. He explained a little loudly that we would be traveling together, leaving the following Tuesday and returning on Saturday.

On the plane, it was easier for me to turn on my interest for him than it was with Mr. Harper because he was much younger and in better physical shape. I was ready. Mid-flight, Stewart turned and kissed me on the lips. "If I haven't told you yet, I think you're stunning, Amanda," he said. He took my hand and placed it on his pants to feel his package. "Very nice," I whispered for him to hear. It is so easy to get to these people with sex, I thought to myself.

He had reserved a suite at the Ritz. From the airport, he told the limo driver to take us through the streets of Paris as much as possible so we could see the sights. The driver went out of his way to go down the Champs-Elysees and in the distance we could see the Eiffel Tower. I was amazed at the spectacular furnishings in the hotel, all gorgeous Louis XIV style, gold trim everywhere. I felt like royalty.

"It's beautiful, isn't it, Amanda," Stewart said.

"I think it's breathtaking, a fantastic backdrop for our wonderful time together," I said.

"I want us to take it slow; get to know each other a little."

"Sure, Stewart, we have a lot of time." (But, I thought, *I'm really only doing what I need.*)

After a hotel massage, we sat and talked in a bar off the lobby, over champagne and caviar (my first).

"You sure know how to treat a lady, Stewart," I said. "It's the best caviar I've ever had. Makes me extra steamy."

"Let's get out of here," he said. I figured we'd go straight back up to the room, but instead he meant for us to go on a walk. We strolled over to the Seine. Stewart wanted to talk about his marriage and kids but I was completely uninterested and had a hard time masking my boredom. I was here to drink champagne, have sex, and enjoy the high life. There wasn't any point in his trying to share his thoughts and emotions with me. I tried to get him to look at the beautiful lights at night on Notre Dame behind us, and the Eiffel Tower in the distance ahead, like the other lovers walking around us. But the romantic views and mood didn't seem to stir anything in Stewart.

When he finally stopped walking, I made the first move. I pulled him close and kissed him on the mouth. I began rubbing him through his clothes. His breathing and pulse increased. I waited until finally he insisted we go back to the hotel. Stewart was slow when we arrived. I removed my clothes and exposed my white garter. He looked but didn't say a word. Instead, he lay next to me and looked up at the hotel ceiling. I became slightly annoyed and decided I had to take control. I moved on top, stimulating him until I could feel him get hard. Within minutes, I felt him ejaculate inside of me.

The next night was the same. I did everything I could to get him into it, but he was suffering from guilt. *I'm glad I don't have that problem*, I said to myself. On the last night, just for a second I started to take out scissors from my purse. I so badly wanted to stab him, thinking of a hundred scenarios of how I could easily cover it up, but I stopped myself. This was the closest I had come to physically hurting someone since Mother told everyone I had a disease.

He was a waste of my time; he hadn't bought me anything and each time we did it, he turned away as if he found having sex with me reprehensible. On that last night, after he finally stopped talking and went to sleep, I pulled a piece of stationery from the desk drawer and wrote a letter to his wife: *'Dear Mrs. Anderson, I just spent the last three nights with your husband, Stewart, and you should work on his manners. Not only did he not thank me for making him come inside of me—something he needed badly by the way—but he didn't compliment my sexy lingerie, something he's probably never seen. Signed, your husband's EX-girlfriend.'* I snuck downstairs and dropped it in the hotel mailbox. (I had his home address—as well as that of all the senior partners—memorized from files at work, a little mental exercise of mine.)

The next morning, on our way back to the airport, Stewart had the limo stop at the Louvre so we could get a glimpse of the Mona Lisa. We were standing in front of the painting when Stewart turned to me and professed I was the most beautiful woman he had ever held in his arms. He whispered that he would leave his wife and kids for me, if I gave him the word. But Stewart was too sensitive. He was a pathetic crier; there had been so many times I wanted to cut out his tongue so he would shut up.

I never received any salary bump from my time with Stewart—although I did hear that his wife left him, which was some satisfaction—so I moved up the chain of men. I tried Rob, who took me to Venice, for some fabulous shopping. I got great stuff, but still no promotion.

A few months later, I worked on Scott. We went to a seriously posh resort in Santa Catarina, Brazil. And while he was generous, like Rob, he was awkward at sex. I heard later, after we went back, that he was gay and had only been experimenting with me. Shit, I was so worried that I got a disease, but I ended up being okay, just pissed, at him, at those around me who hadn't told me, and at myself. I had gotten lax with my 'gaydar' once again. I thought of delicious ways of messing with Scott but there was no point because he didn't have anything I wanted.

The game was getting a bit tedious, and while I did get my salary nearly doubled again over the next couple of years, I didn't get a promotion in title. My department functioned well with few errors. I met a lot of men outside the firm through the company investigations, but none of them interested me. Occasionally I went out with colleagues to the finer restaurants, bars, clubs and events that Manhattan had to offer, but generally, I was okay to just go home to my beautiful condo, sip fine wine, and contemplate my next moves and my bright future.

I was tired of sleeping with the mostly older men above me, so I decided to try out someone younger. My latest hire was Marshall, a paralegal I assigned to handle white-collar crime. Six feet tall with boyish looks, he was a sight in a three piece suit. I was determined to have him. I told him his wife was lovely, but that I was patient. After almost a year, I wore him down. He didn't have the means yet to spend like the other more senior attorneys I had been with, so he took me to Colorado instead. We stayed at the Broadmoor, which was nice, even if it wasn't the level to which I had become accustomed. I was actually looking forward to some good, vigorous sex, but the first night it became apparent that good-looking married Marshall had a severe cocaine problem. He poured half a small plastic bag on top of my naked body and snorted so much, he started to get a little crazy. He managed to finally get off after an hour of pounding and thrusting. That didn't bother me as much as him taking off in the middle of the night, leaving me to pay the hotel bill. He was really hooked on the stuff.

After six years at the firm, I managed to sleep with over a dozen of the men. I call them my conquests. *Not many people can brag about that*, I told myself. I had been to over ten countries and accumulated thousands of dollars in designer clothes and jewelry. The idea of travel still excited me, although sex had become so trivial, it was as easy (and boring) as pouring a glass of milk. I didn't have the hang ups others did about putting out.

I had some trips with repeat partners, mainly so I could go to new and interesting places, although that started becoming exhausting on some level. It wasn't new for them anymore. It was mostly drunk sex. Then some would actually insult me. I got tired of being told I was all used up and cold inside or was only good for one thing. What these smart, educated men didn't realize is that I was using them; I was getting what I wanted, and I didn't care about them or what they thought or called me.

Then one day, Walter, an old esteemed client of the firm came to town. He was particularly close to Mr. Harper, who I assume had told him about me. Walter was in his seventies with about the same build as Mr. Harper, but he had an unattractive hook-nose that looked like a pirate's. It didn't take me long to realize the potential here, of my being worth more to the firm; I could bring money in by satisfying their biggest client. So I laid it on when Mr. Harper brought him by for an introduction. Sure enough, he proposed we take a little trip together the next weekend.

I decided he would be my last trip for a while. The flight to Buenos Aires took thirteen hours because of high winds. His bad breath and snoring distracted me from reading my Anne Rice novel.

When we arrived to the hotel room, Walter wanted to have sex immediately. I was tired from the flight and needed to freshen up.

"Come over here, bitch. I heard you like it rough," he blurted as he reached for my arm.

In an instant, I felt a sting to the left side of my face. Slapped to the floor, I looked up at him, holding my cheek. I struggled to catch my breath. "Walter, you're a piece of shit," I said, choking.

Before I could move, Walter grabbed my throat with his right hand and pushed my head down against the hardwood floor.

"You're a whore, Amanda. Yeah, you're pretty all right, but still a whore, not a bit sexy to me. You're an empty soul, and from what I heard, you don't satisfy anyone but yourself."

I couldn't breathe, I couldn't move. Struggling, to push his hand off, I could feel him touching my breasts under my bra. "Don't you have something for me?" he asked, shifting his hand quickly under my skirt. "Is it under here?"

Walter slipped his fingers inside my panties and began rubbing around my privates.

"Damn you Walter." I squirmed. "Leave me alone." But I couldn't fight him off.

Walter was strong for his age. He managed to lift my skirt and started to pull down my panties.

"Let me go," I insisted, pushing him away with both of my hands.

"I'm not done with you yet," he said, releasing my neck. As he stood up, I caught my breath. "I'll be back and you'd better be in the mood," he said. Then he turned and walked toward the door, slamming it behind him.

Shaking, I stood up slowly holding on to my neck. I walked into the bathroom to place a cool damp cloth under my chin to ease the pain. I sat on the toilet staring down at the floor shocked at Walter's behavior knowing I needed to leave in a hurry. I started to relieve myself, when I noticed Walter had left his pair of high-priced Italian leather shoes. I moved myself above one, then the other, and defecated.

I quickly grabbed my suitcase and rushed out of the hotel for the airport to get a flight. The $150 bottles of champagne and trips to designer stores with drunken, wasted, fat, smelly men were over.

On Monday morning at the office, Marshall stopped in to drop off some files. I was still upset with him for stiffing me with the Broadmoor hotel bill.

"Nice to see you, Ms. Preston, I hope you had another wonderful vacation," he said with a smirk.

"Thank you," I said glancing to the page bottom. Sure enough, I noticed the numbers were deleted. I was already suspicious of him, so earlier I arranged to have copies of all correspondence mailed to me privately. I admired his plan; it was the same one I had used on Melinda. But I was ten steps ahead of him and everyone else. My plan was to surreptitiously leak word of his cocaine problem, and then fire him. Just the thought of it made me smile.

My reverie was quickly interrupted by Eileen, Mr. Harper's secretary. "Mr. Harper would like to see you, Ms. Preston."

I hurried to Mr. Harper's office. "How are you today sir?" I asked as I stepped into his office.

"Please have a seat, Ms. Preston. Beautiful day, isn't it?"

"Yes, sir, it is," I responded.

"I heard you and Walter had one hell of a time. Last time I saw him, he was still cleaning out his damn shoes; he really loves those Italian shoes you know," he said, with a laugh. "Now, Ms. Preston, that's not something someone who is sane does to another person, is it? We all know you're a little crazy around here, but we put up with you because, well, I'm sure you've figured out why. You've been useful to many of us."

I stared directly at him as Mr. Harper reached into his desk drawer and took out a disc. "I have to hand it to you

Ms. Preston; I've been in this business close to fifty years and I've never seen anyone as cunning as you. I overlooked this—video of you sabotaging Melinda all those years ago—but unfortunately for you I just can't overlook what you did to my friend and our client, Walter."

"You are fired, Ms. Preston."

CHAPTER 12

THE SPIRAL

I DUG MY NOSE DEEPER INTO THE STALE DIRTY BLANKETS OF the cheap hotel bed, slowly opening my right eye to catch a glimpse of the man lying next to me. Still slightly intoxicated, I detected a foul smell in the room. I stared sideways for a moment at the brown discolored end table with two empty bottles of tequila, a black plastic ashtray full of cigarette butts and a bottle of cheap Merlot. *Where is this?* I wondered. Then a man's face became clear. *Oh, okay,* I thought for a moment.

Who was he? The bartender? A co-worker? No, couldn't have been; I didn't have a job. My mind was dulled, and I couldn't sit up. By this time, the stench was unbearable. I lifted the blanket only to unleash the source. It was coming from the man lying next to me. A rotten cologne, Aramis, maybe it was that—no, it was ass, mixed with the putrid smell of stale cigarette smoke. I began to feel ill as I smelled my hands; the stink had rubbed off on me. I must have rolled in dog shit I thought to myself. Slowly, I turned onto my left side, away from him only to feel an ache in my abdomen. A flash came of his large stomach pummeling me like a boxer's punching bag. The slobber from his wet kisses hung on me like puke, giving me several instances of throwing up in my mouth. I tried not to think of him inside of me, even as his fluids starting running down my leg. Yuck.

Victoria was sitting at the kitchen table when I walked in. "Third one this month, Amanda. And a real stinker from where I'm sitting," she said, laughing. "Do you have a death wish, sleeping with men you barely know?"

I met Victoria at a yoga retreat in May. At the time, she was looking for a roommate. Since I lost my job, I called her so I could stay in New York while I looked for another job. Victoria was sixty-one, much older than me and fairly big-boned. She was originally Scottish, but had lived in New York City since she and her parents had emigrated decades ago. She ended up with the family's three-bedroom brownstone earlier in the year when her mom passed. Sometimes I could hear her at night still crying for her mother. With no friends to speak of, Victoria was a homebody. She locked herself away to paint pictures of landscapes in a small room she had converted into a studio. She was born well-off and never needed to work for a living.

From day one, Victoria treated me like a child. She would express her opinions on everything, from cooking to men, as part of her day. From what I could tell, she hated men for one reason or another and projected it onto me. I asked her multiple times to stay out of my business, but I couldn't push her because I didn't want to lose the rental deal; it was in a good location. I think I was a needed distraction from her mother's death, and I provided her with vicarious excitement.

Each time she would judge me, I would provoke her back. I would try to ignore her, but she always persisted. We would begin bickering back and forth. It had pretty much become just a dysfunctional form of blunt conversation. I would use my little girl voice that seemed to send her to oblivion. I was determined to keep this $300-a-month room, so I didn't care what she told me.

"Who was it this time?" Victoria asked.

"Don't know, don't care," I said.

"If you keep giving it away, Amanda, you're going to get old, old, old fast. For every man you screw, you get a wrinkle; everybody knows that and no one wants to marry a whore. I bet you can't even satisfy your men anymore. They probably have to get drunk just to do you."

"Maybe I like it, Victoria!" I screamed, just the way she liked me to.

"You have a need to be penetrated, physically and mentally, but you don't know why. You need some serious help girl," Victoria replied laughing.

"It's casual sex, a win-win situation. They think I'm pretty, they pay attention to me, buy me dinner, and in return I do whatever they want," I said. "Who cares!"

Picking up my pace, I headed directly to the shower, closed the door, and removed my clothes.

Victoria's footsteps became louder until they stopped

outside the door.

"You like a man's penis because in your mind you think of it as power."

"I take in every drop, Victoria. I don't waste it. It makes me look younger, and it tastes so good," I yelled, taunting her back.

"If it's so good, then why do you smell so bad?" she replied, laughing loudly. "Are you going to panic again this month because you think you got a disease? Self-destructive is what you are Amanda," she said as the shower stopped.

"Maybe I have a death wish, low self-esteem or something, Victoria. It's just who I am."

Finally, I heard Victoria go back out to the kitchen. I performed the daily routine of transforming myself. Still had all my fancy makeup that worked wonders every time. I quietly slipped my ruined panties into my purse and, careful to avoid Victoria, walked lightly out the door. I planned to throw them out in a nearby dumpster on my way past Chez Renee, a small French restaurant I liked to visit. It was unlikely I would be wearing them again.

I took the subway for the fifteen-minute ride to La Perla.

Standing next to others waiting for the train doors to open, I whispered aloud, "Mind the gap, mind the gap." Confused, I tried to recall where I had heard the phrase, before stepping into the crowded train car. As it started moving, I focused on a sign that advertised Chinese food. They offered free fortune cookies with any takeout order. When the train started moving, I began to feel weak and light-headed. I felt dizzy for a moment, struggling to get my bearings. A sudden flash of memory came as I caught a glimpse of my reflection in the window glass. In the reflection was the figure of a handsome older man standing behind me. He had black shiny hair and was speaking to me. His deep blue eyes startled me, but he looked familiar. Suddenly, his arms reached out to touch my shoulder. "Do I know you?" I asked quietly. "Who are you?" When the train slowed, I grabbed onto the bar, when I looked back at the window, the image had disappeared.

I quickly exited through the crowd up the steps to street level. He was nowhere to be seen. I took a deep breath, and continued down the sidewalk.

From a distance, I waved to Albert as I approached the store.

"Good afternoon, Amanda. Welcome back to La Perla. You look beautiful as usual."

"Thank you, Albert. Isn't it great weather we're having today?" I said.

"Absolutely," he replied.

My favorite lingerie greeted me as I entered the store. It was so nice to feel fancy, pampered and European. My trademark for years, I knew I looked good all under, and had lots of opportunity to show that off. The fabrics were sensational, and their styles sexy and outrageous, like me. Today, I had a mission: to replace my ruined green panties with a more chic red pair. La Perla was my weakness. After a two-hour visit, I settled on a blue lace demi-bra and a maroon satin one. I also picked out a pair of bright yellow Brazilian panties with a price tag of $155.

"Shall I add the items to your bill Amanda?" Albert asked nicely.

"Yes, Albert." I said, walking away.

Victoria was out when I returned. Grocery day for her was Sunday when there were end-of-week discounts. I hung the two new bras in my closet next to my red blouse. Kneeling to place my shoes in my under-bed storage, I began to perspire, followed by another bout of confusion.

A quick visit to the free clinic the next day confirmed I had an STD. "An advanced stage of gonorrhea," the doctor said. I was forced to provide a list of partners from the last six months—I lost count at thirteen. Luckily (for them) I had most of their numbers. Then I thought to add one more to the list I gave the doctor. He was the husband of one of my old colleagues at work. I hadn't actually done him, but one of my snitches had informed me that she started a rumor about me at work, so I added him as one of my sexual partners. *That should teach her not to spread gossip about me*, I thought.

The doctor lectured me for not using condoms, and he warned of other diseases. Mine was easily treatable with antibiotics and several days of rest.

I tried to get rest but I kept getting calls from the men who were upset for being contacted by the Department of

Health to go in for a test. The calls continued. I received threats from a one-night stand I met at bar. *Talk about bad judgment on my part with that guy*, I thought. I just told every one of them to get screwed. A salesman named Dan who I met while looking at a Harley Davidson banged on our door during the middle of the night, yelling that I ruined his life. I had forgotten that Dan and I hadn't seen each other in at least a year. I had given the police most of the telephone numbers of men on my phone and I guess it included him. He kept saying he was going to kill me until Victoria confronted him with the threat of calling the police.

It was constant drama for the next several days; so many vicious messages were left on my answering machine - from both men and women—that I finally unplugged it. It got so bad, that on Saturday night, while a couple of girls and I were hooking up with some guys at Bourquet. One of the exes Ken, came toward me. He was so hot. Then he started yelling, "Amanda, you stupid bitch. My wife just left me. You're a crazy psycho. You're not even a good piece of ass. You're a disease-carrying whore!"

He was so mad, I hurried out the side door and he started chasing me. The heel on my left shoe broke off. I stopped, grabbed it and ran barefoot across the parking lot. In the background I could hear people yelling, "Get her! Get her!" while the girls looked on in disbelief. Ken finally stopped, probably wondering what he would do if he caught me. *So much for Kathryn's advice that married men are safer*, I thought when I stopped to catch my breath.

The next day, I woke up thinking about the exciting stories Gary told me about Silicon Valley. It was time to make good on the promise I had made to myself, to get back to the west coast and to Silicon Valley. I picked up the newspaper that mentioned tech jobs in northern California. I packed the stuff I cared about, and arranged to send my belongings to a storage unit advertised in Santa Clara. I bought a one-way ticket to San Jose. On the flight, I realized I'd forgotten to let Victoria know I'd left.

I was done with New York.

CHAPTER 13

FAIT ACCOMPLI

THE FLIGHT TO SAN JOSE FROM NEW YORK TOOK NEARLY SIX hours. A taxi dropped me at a local hotel. I sat on the bed physically exhausted at the thought of having to pick up and start over again. I needed to find a way to manage simple things and avoid going through all the drama I did in New York.

New York is the problem, not me, I decided. Most people seemed like extreme empath, useful to a certain extent, but tiresome and repellant in the end. They were more like Mother, suspicious and demonstrative much of the time. Silicon Valley was the right place for me. The way Gary described it. I could feed on the fresh energy and undercurrent of entrepreneurs that infused Silicon Valley.

I stayed up the entire night in my hotel room thinking of how to change my life. If both Dr. Devereau and Dr. Samson thought I could be functional and good, I had to find a way. Flipping through television channels, I came across an early morning talk show that happened to be describing methods to "Increase Your Personal Potential". I took the advice and completed their exercise. I wrote down a list of dos and don'ts from my own life experiences. I came up with do compliment and smile a lot. Do abstain from sex, do pay bills. Do not lie or steal. Do not target others. My list contained ten of both. I pasted it on my bathroom mirror so I could see them every day. I spent the next week combing through the newspapers and sending out resumes. I was confident again. I arranged for a rental car to be delivered to my hotel and found a beauty salon nearby to fix my hair before my job search.

Rosalinda, the Filipina stylist suggested a cut that would detract from the wrinkles on my face. Then she suggested a relative of hers who could quickly come over and complete a Botox treatment for me at a discount.

"Screw you," I whispered, low enough so she couldn't hear. When I left the shop, I thought, *these hair salon people out here can be really cruel.* But deep inside, I worried that maybe Rosalinda had a point.

Her rude comment stayed with me. I couldn't concentrate on my driving. Beauty had always been my strength. If I lost that, how would I survive? Panicked, I began shuffling through my bag for any beauty products I could find. No matter what I did, my youth was fleeting. Was Victoria right? Did each man I slept with give me a wrinkle? I stood in front of the mirror in my room and began marking each wrinkle with a black line; along with the name of each man I had sex with, including Mr. Rousseau. I was running out of space. Desperate, I moved on to a sheet of paper. I could recall at least thirty, but I was sure there were more. There was one year alone I counted fourteen. I took the marker and compared the number of wrinkles to each man, and sure enough, Victoria was right.

I passed up red wine for Jack Daniels that afternoon, and after I was buzzed, I made the mistake of looking back at the mirror. At first I screamed from the black on my face, but even after I washed it off I didn't feel much better; I saw an aged and worn reflection looking back at me. My beautiful soft pale skin had begun to take on a more weathered look. Before I could down another drink, the phone rang.

"Is this Ms. Preston?" the voice asked.

"Yes, I'm Ms. Preston. Can I help you?"

"I'm calling from Metrotech Investments. We received your resume and have need of someone with your skills. I believe we can offer you a salary in the range you are looking for. Can you come in tomorrow at 9:00 for an interview?"

"Yes sir. What is your name?" I wrote it down on my tablet.

I knew once I got in the door, the job would be as good as mine. That snapped me out of my funk. I would have a job, and at a starting pay that I would be able to again buy my $200 an ounce SK-II face cream.

I began my job as a financial analyst the next week. Within three days, I rented a nice little house in the Rose Garden neighborhood. To stay on course, I taped my lists on the bathroom mirror to remind me every day.

Still obsessed with my appearance, It was unclear to me how much longer I would be able to attract influential men without resorting to surgery and needles, both of which I am deathly afraid of. I was not ready to admit defeat. I still had my sociopathic talents I could use to control people, but my looks were my initial power. My hope was that I still had the charm needed to attract a middle-aged man who was well-to-do and could provide for my needs.

I prepared a list of old boyfriends and casual acquaintances. On one side the names of those with potential for marriage and on the other side, not so good. I figured I would try and single out any with whom I thought I could rekindle a relationship. But messages I left were not returned. I was insulted at the inference by a couple who implied that no man wanted to marry a promiscuous woman. *Hey, I'd gotten them into bed easily enough. What's the big difference? Who cares if I'd been with other men? I was offering to choose them, and maybe even permanently. Wasn't that enough? I was the one who decided, not them*, I thought.

Unable to identify a candidate from my past to fulfill my need to settle down, I turned to an actual dating website. I had the looks and could easily manufacture charm on a computer screen; so needless to say, I got a lot of hits. It seemed fairly simple for me to see through their paper facades though.

The man I selected for my first date was Matthew. He was listed as the owner of a winery in Napa Valley. At his request, we did not speak over the telephone and instead he asked for a meeting in Los Gatos at a private villa, to taste some new wines. When I arrived for our appointment, I sat in the main room surrounded by several groups of people. Within minutes, I recognized Matthew from his picture as he stepped out of his Porsche. He looked attractive with blonde hair and a dark pin-striped suit.

I saw something familiar in the look on his face from my seat, but I couldn't pin it down. He resembled someone I had met from Briscoe. As he walked closer to the entrance, he began removing his sunglasses. Through the window glass, I focused on his eyes. They surprised me. Though they were beautiful blue, my senses became alarmed. My mind raced. For a split-second I had a flash of another man's face. I pictured his thoughts. I became startled, I had to look away.

Whatever you do, don't make eye contact, I told myself.

Blood rushed to my head. I felt dizzy and somehow afraid. *If he notices your reaction, he'll feel threatened and then you'll be dead*, I thought without really knowing why. My instincts were sharp and warned me away. I shuddered, unable to think clearly.

I glanced down so Matthew could walk in past me. I rushed out the doors to my car and drove away. The experience left me shaken. I never forgot Dr. Devereau's last statement to me. I had to be careful of people who will exploit me because they can recognize my weakness just as I can in others. I learned as much as I could about them. It turns out that some psychopaths—frequently in the guise of a social worker, police officer or attorney - can be predators. I am used to being the predator. It's dangerous to me when I don't know how to defend myself as the prey.

The problem is that I can't read all of them, but fortunately in this case, I did. I recognized Matthew was a psychopath. It's in their eyes. Blue and green are easier for me to see through; brown and dark eyes are more difficult. A psychopath finds a person like me to be a threat because a sociopath like me can detect their weaknesses and sometimes even their thoughts, so it goes both ways. I wasn't a stalker or killer, but Matthew was dangerous. He was definitely the serial killer type so I moved out of his path.

After that experience, I became extra cautious. I insisted on a video and a phone conversation. I met a couple other men through the site over the next months, but they were lackluster at best. Finally, I met Bob.

We were to meet at Peet's Coffee in downtown Palo Alto, near his office. From his profile, he was thirty-nine and a successful venture capitalist. He claimed he had made millions from start-up companies over the previous years and was still well-positioned for large future stock options. From his voice in our brief phone conversation, I could tell he had a dry sense of humor, but he would be manageable.

I thought of my list on the bathroom mirror of what to do, so Saturday found me just like Mother, right on time waiting near the window of the coffee shop on University

Avenue. I glanced across the street and saw a chic furniture store and jewelry boutique. I watched a young couple with a dog walk by, looking in the windows of both, holding hands and laughing. My mind wandered for a second to how my relationship with Bob might be. *Would we have a dog? What do dogs eat?* I wondered. Next door was a flower shop, a place where I thought I might recognize Bob buying something for our date.

A few minutes later, the door swung open and Bob walked in. He had an assured walk but looked nervously around the coffee shop. With a smile he turned in my direction when I raised my hand to get his attention. He was noticing many of the patrons staring at me. I still had the looks that could garner attention from both men and women.

Bob was close to six feet tall, slender build, with light grayish blonde hair and brown eyes. He was wearing a nice tan suit for a Saturday. I was impressed.

"Are you Amanda?" he asked.

"Here's my little red flag," I said with a smile, "just like we agreed."

Bob had a smug look when he saw me, eyeing me up and down from head to toe as I did him. Finally, he said the magic words: "You are quite the beauty, Amanda. Why on earth would you need a blind date?"

"I wanted to meet someone who can carry on an intelligent conversation," I said.

Before long, Bob and I hit it off. We enjoyed a lovely

dinner at a fancy sushi restaurant nearby. He confided in me, and admitted that he was in search of a wife, one that he could show off and pamper. He felt as though I could be the one. With my list in mind, I complimented him periodically, smiled frequently and never hinted about sex.

The next day Bob picked me up in his Tesla Roadster and we drove to San Francisco to enjoy fresh crab on the wharf. On our third date, Bob made a move. We consummated our relationship at the Fairmont Hotel in San Francisco that evening. Not the best lover, he still had three out of four: money, power, and high prestige potential. He said I charmed him from the moment he saw me sitting at Peet's and he was helpless to fight it.

I began my job at Metrotech as a financial manager while Bob and I socialized and with the help of my daily list, became a real couple. I controlled myself while with Bob and relaxed in my role of just looking good and making polite conversation. Bob lavished presents on me and promised a luxurious lifestyle. We attended various Silicon Valley functions where we were treated as a successful twosome and I hadn't even turned thirty.

It was working. I was following Dr. Devereau and Dr. Samsons advice. I had become functional. I found Bob and he wanted me, like I was his queen. He gave me all I needed and wanted. I was his trophy in the bedroom and on the dance floor and everywhere we went, men stared at me out of the corners of their eyes in hopes of bedding me. They gazed at me across the shoulders of their female partners, moving their lips as if to say *hello beautiful*. I was living the Silicon Valley lifestyle. I was surrounded by powerful well-dressed men and envious women. But I didn't do anything; I stayed true to my goal, which was marriage. Because, as the mirror reminded me daily, I wouldn't be beautiful forever.

CHAPTER 14

MARRIAGE OF SUBJUGATION

MY INTRODUCTION TO BOB'S PARENTS WENT WELL. IT became the starting point for us planning the perfect June wedding. When the date arrived, friends showed up from around the country to offer their congratulations. Bob had many relatives from the Bay Area who attended. He felt sad that my parents died in a car accident when I was a child and I had no family to attend on my behalf.

Sam, Bob's friend, gave me away at the wedding and it was a glorious day. Bob was a man deeply in love. I too had learned the value of treating others well, and figured I was as much in love as I could have been, satisfied that Bob was the nicest person with a heart of gold. It was a world away from Mr. Harper and the slimy attorneys at Briscoe.

During our time together, Bob became my teacher. He never asked me about my life but he showed me every day what it meant to be valued and respected. I was a changed person. My dreams of having to take the bodies out of the closet every night had completely stopped, even though I had never identified the woman. I stopped working and become a society housewife. I even learned to entertain. Bob showered me with fine jewelry, and I had carte blanche to decorate our home however I wanted.

On many evenings, Sam—retired as an engineer from a company in the valley—would stop by for a warm meal prepared by yours truly. I found a new world with Bob, and I became more than just functional. He confessed that I was his valued friend.

There were times when my need to control started to creep back in, but I was able to find satisfaction without being conspicuous. I could target minor people around me, and do little acts of sabotage. I reported our gardener and housekeeper for stealing my jewelry, ensuring they would never work again. When they tried to fight back, I had to get the police involved. Bob always supported me and stayed by my side. My former desire to conquer men by using sex was overshadowed by my obsession to preserve my beauty and prevent wrinkles.

Every year for the seven years of our marriage, Bob and I never missed the New York Giants versus 49ers game. It was our thing. I had lived in New York, and Bob was originally from San Francisco. On our last trip to New York for the game, Bob began to develop stomach pains. He was unable to urinate. His stomach swelled and he was in serious pain. He made it through the game but on our flight back to San Francisco, his condition worsened, and the airline requested an ambulance stand by to transport Bob to the nearest hospital. I held his hand until we reached the hospital. I sat in the waiting room next to a father and son who were anxious for the prognosis of the wife and mother who had been in a serious auto accident. But their pain seemed foreign to me. I began thinking back to when I was fourteen and my little brother asked me why I don't cry.

Looking toward the double swing doors of the emergency room, I stood as Bob's doctor came out. "Mrs. Preston, my name is Dr. Davis. Would you please come with me? I need to ask you some questions." I followed him quickly into his office.

"Does your husband have a history of medical problems?"

"Not that I know of, Dr. Davis," I answered.

"Mrs. Preston, we found what looks to be cancer in your husband's stomach. I'm afraid it's likely that it is quite advanced. We'll do a biopsy of course."

"He has what?" I asked, startled. "Does he know?"

"No, we haven't told him. I'd like you to go in with me."

Bob looked much weaker than usual as he lay in the hospital bed and he had a blank stare.

"What is it? Is it serious, Doctor?" Bob anxiously asked.

"Yes, Mr. Patterson, it looks like you may have stomach cancer, and it appears to have spread to a few other parts of your body. We will continue to run some tests, but I wanted you to know as soon as possible, that it's not looking very good. I am very sorry."

Bob grabbed my hand and began wailing. It was just like

Mother when I told her about Thomas. *I understand now, Mother*, I said to myself as Bob clasped my hand.

"I'm so very sorry, Bob," I said, with a soft hug.

After a few minutes, Bob composed himself. "How much time do I have, Doctor?" he asked.

"Probably weeks Bob maybe a month or two at the most." I suggest you and your wife get your things in order and try to enjoy the time you have left; take a trip or something."

Bob turned away from Dr. Davis and me, so we wouldn't see his face. I thought I felt something for a moment, but there were no tears. The truth is, all I could think about was myself.

The swelling never went down. His condition never improved even with all the medications. Bob never left the hospital. I stayed with him day and night, until he fell into a coma. Within five days Bob was gone.

Sam came by during the last few hours along with Bob's parents to say goodbye. Prior to our getting together, Bob had appointed Sam to handle everything should he pass away. Only minimal changes were made to his will when we married.

Bob requested he be cremated and that a picture of him and me always sit next to the urn. After the funeral, I stayed at our house, wandering around as if I was in a trance, thinking I would see him. It felt strange—he was gone and I was alone again. I sensed the loss. I felt an urge, and picked up the phone. I dialed Mother. "Hello, hello," I said, I could hear someone breathing on the other end but then the phone went dead.

Within a couple of days, I received a phone call from Bob's attorney, Mr. Sheldon, asking me to come to his office to pick up a copy of the will. Sam picked me up on a Friday, a week after Bob's passing, and we headed to the attorney's office in San Francisco. Mr. Sheldon greeted us at the door, and offered his condolences. He seated us and got right to the point.

"Ms. Preston, I understand you kept your maiden name so a check will be made out to you, Amanda Preston, in the amount of $250,000. Any sentimental belongings you desire from the home are of course yours to keep, but the house is to be sold within ninety days. The proceeds will be used to pay additional outstanding expenses," he said. Bob had kept me entirely out of all financial dealings but he had always led me to believe that we had millions.

I went home, and the next week packed up most of his things to send to specific people he named in his will. I spent several hours trying to understand the concept of what sentimental belongings were or that I might want.

Still confused over the whole experience, I had a sense of loneliness unsure of where to go. I moved out a little over two months later, after the holidays, as the house was being prepared for sale. I found a small cottage to rent in Atherton, less than twenty-five minutes north, from Palo Alto, where Bob and I had created the only 'normal' life I had known.

My new place was cute and accommodated most of the nice furnishings that I accumulated with Bob during our marriage. I expected I would once again be applying for a job, but didn't need to worry about money for a while.

CHAPTER 15

FALSE ARREST

THE DEAFENING KNOCK AT THE DOOR SCARED THE HELL OUT of me. I leaped out of bed, quickly throwing on my jeans and blouse.

"Who is it?" I asked still dazed.

"Open up, Ms. Preston," the male voice responded.

"Who are you? If you don't leave, I'll call the police."

"This is Officer Van Sommers from the Police Department and I have a warrant for your arrest."

"What? What are you talking about," I asked, choking up. "What is the charge, Officer?"

"Fraud, Ms. Preston."

"Is this a joke?" I shouted. "My husband just died. I'm not opening the door, I'm calling the police."

"I *am* the police. You have three minutes to open the door, or we will break it down. I am holding my ID so you can see it."

My mind suddenly started racing. What was I supposed to do? I was thirty-six years old and I had three minutes or I might be shot and killed.

"I, I can't see your ID," I responded in a panicked voice.

Through the side window, I could see a female officer approaching the front door.

"Ms. Preston, this is Officer Kate Jenkins. Please open the door. We have a warrant to search the premises and bring you in. Please don't resist. If you do, we will have to use force. This is your last warning," she said forcefully.

"I want to talk to somebody else," I replied. "I haven't done anything wrong."

Scrambling to get the phone, I dialed Mother: "The police are here, and they want to arrest me. Help me, help me!" I begged. It was quiet on the other end, but I could hear noises so I knew she was there, until.........click, then the tone went dead.

I grabbed my mace and leaned against the door. "Are you going to shoot me?" I hollered.

"A court order has been filed charging you with fraud." Officer Jenkins replied. "It states right here that you must come with us. You need to open the door, lady, or this will get real ugly."

"Who's doing this to me," I screamed. I quickly thought back to people I had wronged. "Is it Walter? Is it him? Is it because of what I did to his shoes?"

I began dialing the phone again. "Brenda, Brenda, it's me, Amanda, from next door. There are police here, wrongfully accusing me of things. Help me, call a lawyer for me, please. Hurry," I begged.

"Amanda, I don't even know you. Don't bother me," she replied and hung up.

I peeped again through the side window. I could see who must have been Officer Sommers directing the other officers to surround my house.

"I am holding the court order in my hand, Ms. Preston. Come out and let us do our jobs," he insisted.

Feeling faint, overwhelming panic began to set in. I couldn't gain back control, and a sudden pain cut through my brain like a hot iron. My trigger was being set off forewarning me. My mind went blank. I put my hands on my ears, as if to hold up my head. *What is this? What is happening?* I thought.

I was too late.

The next moment, I was in Idaho wandering on my grandmother's farm, picking ripened peaches from the tree next to her front porch. From a distance, I could see Grandma Preston sitting on a stool separating the peaches. *Aren't they sweet, Grandma?* I said. *Can I take some to bake a peach cobbler for dinner, please?*

Of course you can dear, she said.

I opened the oven door: along with the hot blast came the heavenly scent. I breathed it in. *I love your new tablecloth, Grandma.*

Do you, Amanda? You're so sweet, the best.

Grandma always said I was her favorite.

Grandma served another piece of peach cobbler onto my plate, and set it down on the red-checkered tablecloth.

I dug in with my fork; it was soft and mushy. As I bit down, a sound began cutting through me like an ambulance siren in my head.

Before I realized what was happening, a hand was clamped on the back of my neck forcing me to the floor. It was Officer Jenkins.

"Don't make a move, Ms. Preston," she demanded.

She held my face pressed sideways on the tile. I opened my eyes briefly only to see my own blood seeping out from my nose into a puddle. Officer Jenkins released her grip and pulled my arms backward. The loud sound of metal snapping closed simultaneously stung my wrists.

"Someone help me," I moaned, trying to lift my head.

"Ms. Preston, is there someone else here in the house with you? Who were you talking to?" When I didn't speak, Officer Jenkins yelled, "Answer my question!"

After a search by other officers revealed nothing, Officer Jenkins removed her boot from my neck. Struggling to wipe the blood from my mouth, I pleaded, "Help me, help me. Please, don't take me to jail. I don't want to see Thomas. I want my mother."

"Ms. Preston, we asked you to come out. Look at what you made us do."

Then Officer Sommers spoke up, "Do you understand you have the right to remain silent Ms. Preston?" he asked. "Pay attention when I'm talking to you!" he yelled.

I nodded yes.

Then Officer Sommers paused to put on his dark sunglasses and comb his hair back. Jenkins released her boot, and he reached down and pulled me up by the handcuffs. I held on to him but the pain was unbearable.

"Hurry up, Ms. Preston," he said, pushing me toward the front door. "Better walk the rest of the way on your own."

When we walked outside the front door, I could see several officers waiting along with Brenda among the people watching.

"Face the car, Ms. Preston," he ordered.

Without warning, I felt my legs fall under me. The force of Officer Sommers' steel flashlight hit the back of my legs. "Uh…..no," I screamed. Before I fell, he jerked me upward and leaned me up against the car. His face moved right up close to mine. I could see deep rage in his eyes.

"You're a beautiful woman Ms. Preston. Sometimes cooperation goes a long way in our business; I sure don't want to damage your Hollywood looks. I only wish I had time to take care of you myself, but I'm going to have to send you with my friend, Officer Drake. He really knows how to treat a woman," he said laughing.

Pulling me by my left arm, Officer Sommers threw me into Drake's patrol car.

Trying to wipe the blood from my nose with my shoulder, I sat up staring straight ahead. Reality was starting to sink in as I found myself sitting handcuffed in the back of the patrol car. I was breaking. "Where are you, Bob? Mother? I need you," I whimpered. "You said you would always be there for me no matter what…"

CHAPTER 16

CODE RED

"I'M OFFICER DRAKE, MS. PRESTON. I WAS JUST INFORMED BY dispatch there is no room for you in the Atherton jail."

"Where are you taking me, Officer?" I insisted.

"To Sacramento County," he replied, matter-of-factly.

"But it's over two hours away. Why are you taking me so far away? My family is on their way here, my dad, my mother. I can't get any help over there."

"That's the idea," I heard Officer Drake say in a low voice.

"Don't worry, Ms. Preston, we have more than enough time for the trip. There's no hurry, just sit back and enjoy the ride. As long as we get along, there will be no problem."

Officer Drake drove fast out of the city as the buildings distanced behind us.

My guard was up, something didn't seem right. *I can report him and file harassment if he touches me*, I told myself.

"I'm not afraid of you, Officer," I warned, struggling to speak through my neck injury. "What did I do to cause the police to treat me like this?" I asked. "Can't you help me? Can I use your cell phone? I need to call my parents.

Please understand."

"Look, Ms. Preston," he said, reaching to turn off his police radio. "I'd like to think we can be friends. You know, close friends. After all, you and I are almost on a date. Do you mind if I call you Amanda? Then it'll sound more like a date, right?"

This is bad, I thought to myself. Every sign told me I was in trouble. I was powerless. What fraud? Was this even real? And there was another, more pressing problem: this officer wanted something from me and I needed to think.

I know how these cops operate, I thought. I dated a police officer years ago, before I met Bob. He worked in this same police department and told me about other cops steeling drugs and then covering up for each other. He would constantly talk about corruption. He bragged how one of his friends raped a girl at a convenience store in the back office and then when it went to trial, they all showed up in uniform and scared the girl into dropping all the charges. Am I in that girls shoes, is this now staring me right in the face? Wait, I remember something he mentioned about a police code, number seven maybe? It was something like 'protect your brothers at all costs.' *Protect them if they commit rape? Even murder? Who knows how far this goes*, I thought. *But wait, couldn't I claim to somehow be part of them in a way? Yeah, maybe that's how I get out of this situation. They all know each other right?* It was my only chance to save myself.

From somewhere deep inside of me, I managed to say

the words to Officer Drake, "I don't think Jeff Riley would want any harm to come to me, Officer Drake. You know, you touching me. It wouldn't be smart."

"Oh, were you Jeff's girl?" he asked, surprised.

"Yes, Officer Drake, we were together a few years ago for quite a while, very close. Aren't you supposed to protect your own, you know, Code 7? You could get in a lot of trouble, Officer; I wouldn't want you to lose your job."

"Nice try. Code 7 doesn't apply here, Amanda. No problem; we can have a good time. Jeff and I have an understanding. I gave him Gloria, now I get you."

Stunned by his response, I shrieked "You're lying!"

"Who do you think got me started?" he said laughingly loudly.

I hesitated to reply. Officer Drake was not afraid of me. His badge gave him the power to do whatever he wished. He was in control and I could feel the police vehicle slowing down as we turned a wide curve in the road. It had been an hour and a half, and there was nothing around. He was looking for a place to pull over. If that happened, he would surely force me to have sex with him.

"Why are you slowing the car down?" I asked worriedly.

"It's dark, and I figure you and I need to talk about how I can help you when we get to the jail. The judge and I are friends and I can talk to him. If you play ball with me, you can be on your way home by nine o'clock in the morning."

By now, there was no doubt what Officer Drake wanted. I

knew from the moment he picked me up in Atherton. *You'll have to rape me, I thought, you arrogant SOB. You're not going to take me without a fight.* My mind wandered so as not to think of my impending doom. I thought about how great my marriage to Bob was, and how I had stayed true to him. The thought of being touched by a stranger was horrifying; but this pig also disgusted me. *Do I dare push this? He won't do anything to me as long as he knows people will see me at the jail, right? Mother is coming to meet me; I had heard her on the other end of the phone. She'll figure out where I am and bring the best attorney in the state who will have me out by morning, before Officer Drake says he would get me out.*

"I have a lawyer, Office Drake," I announced. "He's meeting us at the jail. He'll have me out tomorrow morning. He's a mean one. When you meet him, he's going to want to know everything about you."

He stayed quiet. I noticed Officer Drake's breathing slightly change. It worked. He must have realized it was too dangerous. Relieved, I sat back, closed my eyes and relaxed onto the seat.

Officer Drake continued to slow the car, looking to his right as though he was patrolling the vicinity. I sat upright to show that my confidence was not shaken by him. But then Officer Drake signaled and pulled over to the right onto a gravel lot. At first glance, I saw picnic tables; the place appeared to be a rest area. On the outside, I maintained my stance, but inside, I could feel my blood draining from my body. "Why are we stopping?" I asked abruptly.

"Just needing a break, Ms. Preston, Relax, I'll be back in just a minute."

He stepped out of the car and stood looking around. I stared out in his direction, I could see an area littered with garbage, old tires, and discarded mattresses.

With a deep sigh of relief, I thought, *Oh he just needs to relieve himself.* I watched him until he disappeared into the dark. I looked around, listening to the police radio—it sounded like several officers were being dispatched to a neighborhood fight.

It seemed peculiar. I looked up and the bright beam from the moonlight offered me some solace as a giant beacon of good. Finally, when I could see Officer Drake's large shadow returning to the car. *Good*, I thought, *let's get out of here so I can see Mother.* Then to my surprise, Officer Drake clumsily shifted his large torso in my direction and headed to the back door to where I was seated.

CHAPTER 17

WHEN BRUTALITY HAS NO NAME

OFFICER DRAKE PULLED THE BACK DOOR OPEN WITH A force that could have bent the hinges. I dared not look up at him. Instead I turned to look directly at the trees in the distance. A quick chill came over me when I glimpsed up at the glass. The combination of the moonlight and the reflection of the car window displayed a large disproportionate face behind me. I quickly dropped my head to bury myself on the seat when I felt the wet of his lips moving around the back of my neck. I flinched but Officer Drake was quick and jerked me upward until I was facing him. He leaned in close and began licking my forehead with his sandpaper tongue long enough for me to feel his black wiry unibrow. I winced at the stench of the putrid decay that emanated from his nose and mouth. His lips pushed to mine until I could taste the rot of his spit.

He took a deep breath, then whispered in my ear, "Get out of the car, Ms. Preston."

I choked up, and grabbed onto the seat belt latch under me. I held on to it tightly and slumped sideways into a fetal position to protect myself.

"If you fight me, I will drag you out by your damn hair!" he shouted.

I screamed as loudly as I could, but it didn't matter. Officer Drake grabbed my hair and rolled it into a ball. "Nobody can hear you Amanda." I could see the key to the handcuffs secured to the right side of his belt, and there was nothing I could do. There was nowhere for me to go. I was trapped.

"Please don't—not that," I begged.

"It's better if you cooperate. You're going to do what I want or I'll mess you up."

"What?" I said gasping. "I—"

Suddenly I felt a crack to the side of my face. My eyes fluttered and I felt my body go limp. Somehow I had fallen and my head was pinned on the floor mat. I began to shake. The earlier breeze now had a strange scent of my blood as it streamed down over my nose and mouth. I had been clubbed by Officer Drake.

Before I could catch my breath, he yanked me out of the back seat and threw me onto the ground with one swift motion. He gripped the top of my hair and dragged me like a rag doll over the dirt and gravel of the parking lot. Sharp rocks pressed into my skin with each pull, embedding deeper and deeper into my legs until we reached the grass and trees.

As the shock began to wear off, I attempted to cry out only to feel a hot jolt against the back of my head as if I had been whiplashed. I began screaming from the excruciating pain.

My upper back felt the sting of a shard of glass pierce my skin. Before I could let out another sound, I felt a chill as my dress was ripped from my body. With my back on the ground, the blood in my eyes became the distraction from seeing what was taking place above me. I screamed, but there was no one who could hear me. With each part of my body being jerked in all directions, his large hands tore my bra and panties to reveal my private areas. Each time I tried to fight, he slapped me across my stomach. It felt as though every organ in my body could explode. He spread my legs and laid on me; it felt like I was chained to concrete hooks. I couldn't move.

In an instant, I felt a sharp pain between my thighs. The force of his penetration quickly became a jabbing, throbbing that radiated to my brain. With each violent thrust, the shard of glass and handcuffs dug into me. I couldn't make a sound, I couldn't breathe. My legs had been opened wider than humanly possible that I felt as though I would break in half. The large weight of him on top of me was suffocating. I thought of my life and how I would die. Then the thrusts became slower and I began to feel some relief. As Officer Drake reached ejaculation, his loud raspy moans stopped followed by the warmth of his fluid entering my body.

Officer Drake stood to pull his pants up. My body was finally relieved of the heavy weight on my tiny frame. I lay flat as a corpse, bloodied, stained, and disfigured, like someone mangled by the steel of a tractor blade. In my attempt to move, the glass in my back had lodged in deeper. A cold numbness came over me. It felt as if my naked lifeless body had been drained but was somehow still inhabited by a mindless soul and left to die.

The nighttime breeze brought more cold, as if to suck away the remainder of my life.

My ears detected no words, no noise, not even the usual familiar cracking sounds of tree branches in the wind, as if nature itself remained silent stunned to have born witness to the violence forced upon me by Officer Drake. My blood soaked eyes opened blurred still stinging unable to focus. In the sky above I thought I could make out the Big Dipper. I pictured myself back in my bed, where I could look up through the skylight at the stars. My back numbed and even the shard didn't hurt so much anymore.

Suddenly, I heard a vehicle's tires slide on the gravel and the sound of a police radio in the distance. Broken, I rolled to the side and tried to sit up, bringing my legs slowly, stiffly together. I tried to see through to the clearing. Directly in front were two police officers laughing with Officer Drake. Panicked that he may have called them to finish me off, I quickly grabbed onto the nearby weeds and began pulling to hide myself in the bushes. The pain in my abdomen worsened until I had to lay my head down. I looked down at my feet and saw my clothes sitting on the grass ripped to shreds. I tried to get up to run or turn myself around to grab the clothes, but I just couldn't.

I must have let out a sound, because when I looked up, Officer Drake was standing right above me. "Where do you think you're going Ms. Preston?" he smirked.

I heard the sound of engines taking off in the gravel, leaving us in a trail of dust.

Officer Drake handed me an orange one-piece prisoner jumpsuit with the number 777 on the back. "Put this on," he said.

"I can't move," I said crying. "I'm bleeding and I think my leg is broken. You really hurt me."

"You're not hurt, Ms. Preston. Take this water bottle and wash yourself. Then put on the suit, or I'm going to have to call my friends and ask if maybe they want some of you." He finally reached down and took off my handcuffs.

Though it was cold, I poured the water onto me. It had a soothing effect.

"Hurry up if you want to see your mother, or I can leave you here and say you jumped out and were now a vegetable. You're in my world now, Ms. Preston, and you will learn that there are worse things than being dead."

Officer Drake was right; I looked down and poured more water to clean the blood and semen from my body.

"Wash yourself down there real good, don't want any evidence," he said.

Holding back tears, I looked up at Officer Drake.

"How many other women have you done this to?"

"You're a crazy lady. Who do you think they're going to believe, me or you?"

CHAPTER 18

EIGHT HOURS ON THE INSIDE

WE ARRIVED AT THE JAIL AFTER MIDNIGHT. OFFICER DRAKE walked me inside through a back door probably to conceal my condition. We were met by a guard standing next to a shiny steel set of black doors.

"Where are her shoes?" the guard asked glaring at Drake.

When Officer Drake failed to respond, he demanded, "Where are her shoes, Drake?"

"Don't know, that's the way I got her."

"You're late."

"Just process this one, Dave."

"The charge is fraud. The order will be here on Monday."

Officer Drake turned to me and winked, and then walked away.

I was led to the back by the guard. The bruising on my neck and arms had begun to show.

"Are you all right, Ms. Preston?" he whispered.

"I just need a minute to sit down," I said.

"Stand here and put on these sandals and change into this orange infirmary uniform," he said. "Tie the back straps, and then you can sit down while I process your paperwork." When he removed my handcuffs I let out a moan. Both of my wrists were cut and had dirt, pebbles and grass embedded under the skin.

The guard went through a lengthy checklist, ending with "Are you pregnant?" I said no.

He came over to my chair, "We're done," he said. "Please stand. I'm going to place you in solitary for tonight, Ms. Preston, so you can get some rest."

"Has any of my family arrived?" I pleaded, even though I knew the likely answer that if someone did come, did find me here, they couldn't have arrived this soon.

"No, Ms. Preston and if they do, they won't be able to see you tonight. Not till tomorrow morning after nine a.m."

The guard watched me as I struggled to stand. On the chair was a smear of blood that had seeped out of me.

We both focused on it for a second.

Without any comment, the guard slowly led me down a long corridor. There was no sound or light except our foot-steps and randomly blinking fluorescents buzzing overhead.

He signaled to another guard in a glass cage to open the door by remote.

"Please step inside, Ms. Preston," the guard said. "Your mattress and cover are folded in the corner."

The door closed behind me with a loud clang. The shock of the ordeal began to set in.

A voice on the intercom came on. "Ms. Preston, for your

safety, you will be monitored twenty-four hours a day by a guard from behind the small window over there. If you need something, please press the red button below."

The small five-by-eight foot cell was solid block with no windows to the outside, only a toilet, a vent and the one-way glass. There was an oddly shaped blue clock high up close to the ceiling on one wall. Weakened from the assault, I stood motionless in the middle of the floor and focused on the wooden sandals at my feet. They had accumulated drops of fresh blood mixed with Officer Drake's semen. The left sandal seemed to have dried yellow stains of mustard left from the previous person.

The forced air in the cell moved my orange uniform from side to side, leaving me feeling even more exposed. I tried to grab the loose edges and hold it onto me better, pausing for a moment to look at the cuts on my wrists from the handcuffs.

The clock showed almost one a.m. Unable to stand much longer, I staggered over to the mattress and collapsed. Thoughts of Mother and Bob faded away as I closed my eyes.

I was awakened by a loud clang, then the hydraulic sound of the door opening. It was one-thirty. I slowly lifted my head to see a black woman probably in her thirties holding a blanket and walking toward the other end of the cell. She climbed onto the top bunk of the four-bed frame. I fell back to sleep.

During the night I heard the opening of the door, again and again. I couldn't gather the strength to look.

The numbing began to subside, but then the pain in my abdomen came to life. I rolled onto my side to find relief. I looked up to see the clock; it was three a.m. An odor of something wet on my mattress caught my attention. I looked closer and was startled to see it was bloodied. I began to scream, "Someone help please. Help me, I'm bleeding!"

Across from me, I could see the other inmates in the beds but none would come to help.

"Help!" I screamed as I stumbled to the small window, frantically pushing the red button. Immediately the door opened and a bright light shined directly at my face.

"Please help me," I cried! "I'm bleeding."

"Move to the center and stand still Ms. Preston," the voice said.

A male guard walked quickly around to my back and placed a band locking my wrists together. The pain was almost unbearable.

"I'm Doctor Stevens. Please stand still, Ms. Preston, while I examine you."

"Are you on your period?" he asked.

"No," I said.

He then directed a guard to bring in a new mattress with a gurney.

Two others helped me onto the mattress as the doctor spread my legs to perform a vaginal examination. I heard him say that I had suffered from a self-inflicted wound.

"Note that in the record," he told one of the guards.

The doctor told me to open my mouth, and stuffed in several pills.

"Swallow these, Ms. Preston. Then we won't need to hear another peep out of you."

They set the mattress, with me on it, on the floor, and took the gurney. The steel door slammed behind them. I dozed off and the last thing I remember was rolling onto my side on the new mattress...

I couldn't sleep, my head began to throb and I moaned as the pain in my body worsened. I began to whimper for Mother. Suddenly, I felt a nudge on my mattress. Petrified to move, I began to panic. Then a soft hand touched my forehead. Calming and soothing, the same way Mother would touch me when I was a little girl when we laid together on the couch. I instantly relaxed, took a deep breath and closed my eyes...

But I awoke again when the opening of doors and pounding from someone on the walls of another cell became louder. I looked down and there was no blood. My back stayed numb and felt as though it had been struck by a large object. I looked up at the clock; it was five a.m. I got up slowly and walked over to the bunks to see the others, but they had already been moved.

With each step, pain shot up my back. I stumbled to the small window and felt my way to press the button.

"I have to see Mother and my lawyer. Please let them know I'm here," I said weakly.

Within minutes, a guard's voice came on the speaker. "No one had called or showed up to check on you, Ms. Preston," he said.

"I need a doctor, I screamed."

Two hours later, the doctor came. The same one who had given me the exam and the medication the night before.

"Why am I in so much pain?" I asked. "Why can't I leave?"

"I'm sorry, Ms. Preston, we are doing all we can for you."

"What about the other women, the ones in here with me?" I sobbed. "Where are they? I want to be with them."

"Ms. Preston, there are no other women here with you. You are in solitary confinement. You have been in the cell alone all night."

Frightened and confused, I broke down and fell to the mattress on the floor.

CHAPTER 19

WHEN VOICES STIR

I COULD BARELY DISCERN THE IMAGE OF A HAND ABOVE ME in the dark as the prick of a needle penetrated my skin. I was vanishing, fading; I must have been sedated.

Lying partially clothed on the mattress, I didn't strain to look any harder. I didn't care. Instead, I hung my head off to feel the cool of the concrete floor. I began counting stars. Bright lights in the distance gave me a sense of peace.

Then a voice.

"You're safe, Amanda," a woman said softly. "Get some rest, my dear. Everything will be fine in the morning."

"Who are you?" I whispered. "Are you my trigger?"

"My name is Melba," the voice responded.

By this time, the other women in the cell began to move closer.

"Why are you here, Melba?"

"Killed my husband. Self-defense it was. He had a bad drug problem, beat me ever'day. Sold ever'thing we had for drugs. Woulda sold the kids too, if I hadn't taken 'em."

"How long have you been here?" I asked.

"'Bout six years now; one more to go," she said. "Rhonda here only has six months left in this hellhole."

A tall red-headed woman came over and sat across from me. The severe acne scarring on her face was extreme. Her hair was a frizzy mess, but I could see that she had a decent body. When she opened her mouth to speak, her breath smelled diseased, like that of a rotting corpse. Her slight drawl was slow and deliberate.

"Needed money for food, so I prostituted here in the valley. Used to walk along Watt Ave. near Orange Grove. My sweet spot, y'know. Sometimes brought me $300 to $400 a night. Had my pimp, had my bling. Always kept my pride. Never let em hurt me. One day, found my pimp was making a play for Shanny, my daughter. Fourteen, would you believe it?"

"What did you do, Rhonda?" I asked.

"I lost it, couldn't control myself. Put a knife in his head, watched it come out the other side. Can't fix that, so here I am. Didn't make no difference, though; Shanny went with another stinkin pimp down on Broadway and 1st working the streets, so that's that. Won't even stop by to visit," she sighed.

I looked up and the other two women had gathered around Melba and Rhonda.

"We all friends here; we take care a each other," Melba said.

I could see Melba's eyes water, as I watched the others give her a hug.

A large-boned blonde woman walked over and kneeled

next to me. "I'm Tina," she said, in a deep gravelly voice using both arms in the form of a gang sign to show off her multiple tattoos.

She put her hand on my forehead to give Melba a rest.

Tina's hand felt like sandpaper as she began moving it across my forehead. I dared not say a word.

"Don't worry. What she said. We'll watch over you Amanda," Tina said.

Tired from the medication, I was managing to talk as long as I didn't move.

"What's your story, Tina?" I asked with interest.

"Had a house, a great life, until a piece of shit hijacked our car, stabbed my husband five times right in front of me. Threw me out of the car at fifty miles an hour and messed up my face." She turned away but I could see it deeply disturbed her.

"I got him later though," she said. "He was coming out of Percy's Bar. Shot him right on the sidewalk, four times: two in the stomach, two in the head, one of those in between the eyes. Was trying to get a fifth one off - one shot for each stab to my husband ya know - when they tackled me from behind. Got caught." She stopped and let out a big sigh.

"Everybody knew I died way before I killed him, though, tried to cut my wrists to make it permanent, but no luck."

Jenn, a five-foot, frail-looking thing with black shoulder-length hair, patted Tina on the back in support. "We all got our reasons for not wantin' to be here, in jail or in life," she said pensively.

My eyes closed when I could no longer resist the full effects of the medication.

Morning came. I awoke as I was being wheeled to the jail hospital.

"My name is Dr. Adler, Ms. Preston. I'm here to change the bandage on your head and remove some glass and a metal object from your upper back. Also, one of our guards reported that you may have been sexually assaulted, so I'll be performing an examination of your vaginal area to check for signs of trauma."

"They already checked me," I muttered. "I want to go home."

Handcuffed to the railing of the bed, Dr. Adler turned my body sideways and inserted a probe inside of me. Unable to move, I felt the sting of yet another needle prick...

When I awoke, Dr. Adler was standing above me.

"Ms. Preston, how do you feel? You've been asleep for two hours. I placed stitches on your head and back, so you will need to be careful for several days. There is also significant injury to your vaginal area. I've given you a shot to prevent infection, but you should abstain from any intercourse for at least a few months to give yourself time to heal."

After Dr. Adler left, I was taken to a staging area where I was to go before Judge Patrick.

"Stand up Ms. Preston, and face the camera up there on the wall," the guard said.

There was a face on the screen.

"Ms. Preston, I am Judge Patrick, the D.A. was pursuing this case against you, but I have received information that at this time your creditors are satisfied that your debt to them has been paid, and they do not wish to press charges. Your case is therefore dismissed, and you are free to go," he said.

The guard provided me with some used clothes and boots. They felt dingy and baggy when I put them on. It was all like some surreal whirlwind. My two days in hell were over.

I walked through the guards' security area. After processing, I tried calling Mother. I couldn't believe I hadn't heard a single word from her. She had to have gotten my message. The phone rang and rang, until it was the answering machine again. I left a message, hung up and waited.

Four hours passed while I sat uncomfortably and waited while guards watched but Mother never called. Finally, a female guard came and offered to take me back to Atherton. We didn't speak the entire way back, but I caught a glimpse of the picnic area where Officer Drake raped me. For a moment I turned to the guard and thought, why bother, Drake was a cop, like all cops, they have all the power and nobody would have believed me anyway.

CHAPTER 20

THE RIDE HOME

TWO HOURS LATER, I WAS DROPPED OFF AT MY HOME IN Atherton. Relieved to smell the fresh cut lawn in front, I kissed the railings as if to say, *I'm home.* It felt as though I had been gone for a year. When I put my key in the lock, it jammed and wouldn't turn. I walked around the outside to the bathroom window to check the screen. It was just as I had left it, off on the bottom just in case. I stuck my head under the frame and hoisted myself inside and into the bathtub. When I turned to step out, I almost lost my breath.

I ran through the house and found that everything was gone, including my ring from Bob and my necklace from Mr. Harper. In total disbelief, I wanted to scream. I held my arms to the side of my head and sunk to the floor. I couldn't bear to look up where my designer clothes used to hang.

Struggling to compose myself, I walked hurriedly the two blocks to my bank. When I walked inside, the date at the front said Thursday, March twelfth. I went directly to the manager. "Sir, my name is Amanda Preston, and I would like to withdraw some money from my account."

"Good afternoon, Ms. Preston. Please have a seat. I will be glad to help," he said.

He pulled up my account on his computer screen and asked for my date of birth.

He paused, with a strained look on his face. "I hate to inform you, Ms. Preston, but your account was seized two days ago and it seems your money went to satisfy your creditors."

"What are you talking about?" I yelled. "What creditors? I have no debt."

"From the list I have here, Ms. Preston, it shows you charged at Gucci for $36,000, La Perla for $61,000, and several others—all in New York."

"When did they find out I had an account here?" I asked.

"A check from Basco Life Insurance for $250,000 was deposited into your account a couple months ago. The system automatically reported your social security number. The creditors must have had a flag with a company that monitors such information. I'm very sorry but someone should have explained this to you."

"Do I have any money left?" I asked.

"Your balance is seventy-one cents."

"Let me have it," I said abruptly.

I walked out into the street only to be met by the hint of the evening chill. I had nothing, and the ordeal with Drake seemed to have drained me of any motivation. I walked back to my house and sat in front on the curb.

Before I could rest, a police car approached me. I became startled until I saw one of the officers was a female.

"What's your name lady?" the patrolman asked.

"Amanda, this is my house," I explained.

"You can't stay here, lady. Unless you are the owner and have a valid title, you are breaking the law. If you don't leave, we will have to arrest you for trespassing."

Not words I wanted to hear. I quickly stood up and started walking away, still in those dingy baggy clothes from the jail. I walked west, toward the hills, away from people. I remembered there was a small stream not too far away where the road formed a bridge. It was only five minutes from my house and a place for me to think. I walked to the bottom of the stream embankment to take a closer look. I sat on an old abandoned refrigerator and looked across at the ripples in the water. The cold air from the wet grass and weeds added to the late winter night's chill. In the dirt below, I noticed an old sweater lying half visible. I reached down and pulled it out. It was rust-colored, with long sleeves and a belt still attached by the rings. I shook the dirt off and put it around my shoulders.

The moon became brighter, and in the distance, it shined on a mother with her children unfolding cardboard onto the moist ground for their bed. Further down, the voice of a man sounded desperate to find someone and was calling out, "Penny, Penny." In another area, there was a scuffle over a blanket between two teens trying to stay warm. There was the noise of a child whimpering just a few feet away that made me uncomfortable.

The moonlight was a beacon for people looking for shelter under the bridge. At times it seemed as though the surrounding bushes came alive from the motion of their footsteps. I had no idea there were this many people without a home around this area. The sound of a woman's screams on the opposite side of the river alerted me that I needed to hide in case I was spotted. I kneeled quietly in a small recess in the grass until I couldn't be seen. I tried to maneuver into a better spot but my body still ached. When the screams from the woman finally stopped, I closed my eyes, more exhausted than I can ever remember.

I shivered, awake, much of the night. Finally when I dozed off, I was awakened by several loud pop, pop, pop sounds further down the river that scared me. I jumped up and ran to a nearby convenience store. I hurried into the restroom and slammed the door behind me. Tired and dirty, I struggled with tissue paper, trying to remove the dirt and grass stains from my pants. I left the restroom quickly and walked back to the curb by my house to wait.

Throughout the next day, people stared while I sat alone in front of my house. I would stay as long as I had to; I wasn't planning to leave without getting my stuff back. I stayed gripping the sweater around me all day until the bitter cold became unbearable. When there was still no sign of the property manager, I headed back toward the bridge to crawl into the same spot for a second night. The trauma of the last week was taking its toll on me and now I was starving. I felt weak and began to think of Mother. *Where was she? And why hadn't she called me?*

Exhausted, I started to close my eyes but couldn't. I was drawn to the constant smell of food cooking at the Italian restaurant on the nearby corner. It was too much to bear. I didn't want to lose my spot but I had no choice. I decided I would rush over, get what I could and eat when I returned. I stood up and hurried to the front of the restaurant. Through the glass, I watched people eating inside much like I'd done only a few days earlier. I went around back; I had to find some food soon. I stared at the dumpster and paused for a second. Feeling weak, I lifted the lid to take a peek inside. There sitting on top as if carefully placed was a mound of pasta primavera mixed with shrimp fettuccini. I reached over and broke off a small branch from a tree and used it to spoon the pasta into a used Styrofoam cup.

Suddenly, I heard a voice yelling in the distance, "Get out of there. That's mine. Get out, get out!" A man wearing a long black coat hobbling on crutches was coming toward me. I took the food, slammed the lid shut, and raced down the alley. I huddled behind a wall until the man was gone. Starved, I took out the tree branch and spooned all of it into my mouth. I felt a lump in my throat and started to gag until finally the food made its way to my stomach. I rushed back to the bridge and slipped into my crevice in the tall grass to try and sleep.

The sounds of people crying in my area were nonstop throughout the night. Annoyed, I picked up a stick and went to a nearby tree where I found a woman who looked like she had been beaten. "Shut up, shut up, just shut up." I yelled, as I pushed the stick to her chest.

Saturday morning came, and I awoke still groggy from the lack of sleep. The cold had weakened my body, and pains in my stomach had increased. I didn't know if it was from not having enough to eat or if my infection had worsened. I walked to the convenience store and bought a cup of coffee with the seventy-one cents from the bank. I took the cup and went back to sit on the curb. I waited all day, but again, no one came. By mid-afternoon, I began to feel delirious and sick. I was desperate; I couldn't sleep another night under the bridge, and my stomach had swollen like Bob's. I had also developed a discharge from a large sore on my leg that resembled a spider bite.

With nowhere else to go, I looked through a phone book and found the address of a local shelter. It was four miles away. I walked as quickly as I could, but it still took me two hours because I got lost. I couldn't see that well, but I got there around five I think. It was already nearly dark. I walked directly to a bin of clothes and scrounged through a pile. I found a heavy green jacket worn at the sleeves, but filled with down to keep me warm at night. I grabbed two thick sweaters, three pairs of pants, and anything else I could carry.

I overheard two men talking about heading over to the food kitchen. Too hungry to think about it, I followed them a few feet into another building where twenty or thirty people were waiting in a line. I stood behind an older man with a little girl by his side. I heard him say he lost his job at a local chip maker start up, and couldn't find anything else. He'd lost his house and wife too. When I finally made it to the food, I picked up my plate and held it for the server behind the glass. The woman on the other side was in her mid-fifties and fit the profile of the giver, the empath with the bleeding heart. I try to stay away from them. *They talk too much and can't keep secrets*, I thought. Oddly, just that little realization about her brought a much-needed spark of confidence back to by beleaguered brain.

"You're new. I haven't seen you here before. What's your name," she asked with a perky voice?

"Amanda," I said.

"My name is Lisa. You're an attractive young woman, not the kind we usually get around here, Amanda. Are you staying in a safe place?"

"I think so," I said. "But I hear a lot of screaming."

"Why don't you stay here tonight? We have an extra bed and you don't have to be scared."

"I'm not scared. Besides, I need to stay closer to home so I can keep checking if the property manager comes back to my house, so I can get my things."

"Well, be careful. There are a lot of bad people," she said.

Yes, I thought, *years ago she might have thought I was one of those bad people.* I got another surge of pride.

I sat at a table in the corner with a place setting for two. I ate the mashed potatoes and gravy in minutes. I placed the small, boxed drink into my new jacket along with the cookie. I had to get back to the bridge before it was too late to claim my spot. With energy from the food, I made the walk back quicker.

When I returned to the bridge, I took the pile of clothes and placed it on the spot where I had been sleeping. It was dark, and I was exhausted from the long walk. I waited until I felt safe and there was no one around to kneel down and rest. The cold didn't feel quite so bad with the clothes. I closed my eyes and fell asleep.

In the night, I was frustrated to be awakened again. This time I felt a tug on my leg. Startled, I opened my eyes and there in front of me was a man lying on the ground with his head at my feet. I jerked my leg away and as I was about to get up and run, he lifted his head and put his finger to his lips for me to stay quiet. He looked up at me with watery eyes and sort of pathetic like Sara did when we were kids. Then all of a sudden, he just turned and rolled onto a mound of grass a few feet away from me. The weeds were tall and I couldn't see him, but I knew he was there. Suddenly, another man, tall and bearded, appeared holding a large knife. The light of the moon shined on the long silver blade with an eerie silence.

He began yelling, "Where are you? I'm going to kill you."

I stayed silent, quiet for my life. The bearded man moved closer to my feet and began to focus in on me, but I was in his shadow so he couldn't see me. Just as I was about to scream, I heard someone speak. "I'm here, if you want me. I'm right here," it said. The crazy man with the blade quickly turned away from me, stepped over the tall grass…and…stabbed, one, two, three, over and over, plunging the knife into the other man's body. The reflection of the blade was like a mirror as he pulled it out of the man dripping streams of blood after each stab. The bearded man raced off holding the large blade at his side, leaving the body gurgling for its last breath. I stayed silent, I could smell his blood in the cold air while he continued moaning, dying. After a few minutes, the gurgling finally stopped and he went quiet. I pulled my sweater over me and closed my eyes to sleep. When dawn came, I grabbed my clothes and rushed to my house.

Within a couple of hours a blue Lexus drove past me and into the driveway. A young dark haired man wearing a black tie stepped out and slowly walked toward me.

"Are you injured, ma'am? Do you want me to call an ambulance?" he asked.

I stood up, as straight and strong as I could. "I'm Amanda Preston," I replied. "I don't need the police, I just want my things."

"But there's blood all over your face and clothes. Are you sure you're not hurt?"

"It isn't mine," I said, wiping the still moist blood from my face. He looked at me strangely, with a little fear behind his eyes but I didn't care.

"Where is my stuff?" I demanded. "I have been waiting here for days," I exclaimed.

"Why didn't you call me?" he asked. "I hope you understand we had no choice but to auction your personal items. You were more than two months past due and your creditors had already given you several breaks."

"How could you take all my stuff?" I shouted. "I'm homeless, I have nothing. You took everything from me."

"Relax Ms. Preston," he replied lowering his voice.

"I have some good news for you. Our company only needed to auction half of your items, which along with your monetary assets, paid off the creditors. A single buyer has already come forward and offered to buy all of your remaining items for $10,000. I have a cashier's check with me. It will help you get back on your feet. Just sign here and the bank over there will cash it for you."

Without hesitation, I took the check, signed and got my money. I called a taxi to take me to the nearest Holiday Inn where I slept on clean fresh sheets after the longest hot shower of my life. The next morning I picked up the San Jose Mercury News to scan the classifieds.

CHAPTER 21

I AM THAT GOOD

"WELCOME TO MADISON FINANCIAL, MS. PRESTON. PLEASE have a seat." I crossed my legs to cover the run on the lower part of my hose.

"My name is Douglas Cruz, I'm the CEO. I am in need of an administrator, so the person we hire will work directly for me. It requires complete discretion, Ms. Preston, mainly because of the amount of confidential information about the clients. I reviewed your resume and it is impressive. Can you elaborate for me why you believe you would be suitable for this job?"

"I'm a team-player and working in finance has always been a passion of mine, Mr. Cruz," I said, putting out the necessary buzzwords. "Above all, I'm loyal, and I have a high degree of respect and integrity. I also have a successful history of working in high-profile jobs."

Although I had said it properly, Mr. Cruz looked at me puzzled. For a half second he recognized something, it wasn't clear, only that his psyche warned him. My tendency to raise this flag in some people had been explained to me, by Dr.

Samson, who had also helped me to know how to get past it. I needed to quickly distract Mr. Cruz.

"This is a wonderful company, Mr. Cruz. Did you move to San Jose, or were you born here?" I asked.

Cruz dismissed his gut feeling. "I was born and raised here, Ms. Preston," he said.

"One more question, Ms. Preston," he continued. We have a very strict no fraternizing policy here at Madison. I assume and hope this doesn't present a problem for you?"

"No sir. I would never, and have never, had a relationship with a co-worker. I don't believe one should be so selfish as to practice that type of behavior, at the expense of the company. You have my word," I said.

The call came with a job offer in two days. I accepted and began the following Monday.

I dressed conservatively on my first day. A below-the-knee red skirt, black silk blouse and pumps. I'm sure I looked horrific in my department store clothes. My shoes barely even had a two-inch heel. I waited for a few minutes at the front desk until Mr. Cruz came to get me. "Welcome aboard, Ms. Preston," he said. He took me for a tour of the department and introduced me as his new administrative assistant to the other six people in the department. Four were men and two were women.

As we walked through, it was obvious Mr. Cruz was well-liked. Charles, an employee in the same division that handled customer complaints, didn't hold back. He stared me up and down, and I felt his heart race when he shook my hand. He was mildly attractive, and the lust in his eyes was apparent. Without knowing much about him, I presumed he would be the office whore if I needed one. I just gave a polite, professional smile, but I let my eyes linger a split second extra to make sure I had hooked him.

I learned quickly that Mr. Cruz had a reputation as a risk taker. Madison considered him their star. He had made the cover as "Man of the Year" on *Community Weekly*, a Silicon Valley magazine, which bolstered Madison's already first rate image. Mr. Cruz was also finalizing financial support from investors to renovate some abandoned buildings in downtown San Jose. The project was on a grand scale and expected to help alleviate the homeless problem by offering affordable housing to the working poor.

Mr. Cruz had an impressive clientele. This enabled me to be privy to confidential information about some of the wealthiest people in Silicon Valley. Mr. Cruz trusted me. Within three months, I became familiar with the entire operation. Mr. Cruz still had not figured me out and he remained cautious. I managed to gain the trust of the other employees in the department though, with simple little gestures like a compliment or a cup of coffee. It was so easy being back in the game. With Charles, an open button on my blouse worked wonders. They all posed no threat to me—but also no challenge to or goal for me - since they were technically subordinates. I already had my sights on what I wanted.

Late on a Friday, Mr. Cruz called me into his office for a private discussion. He presented me with several documents he said I improperly processed, indicating I created a liability for the company.

"I'm concerned, Ms. Preston. This is the second time the issue of confidential documents finding their way into incorrect files has come up. Please take more time to check over your work."

"I'm sorry, it won't happen again," I said.

After a few minutes I watched Mr. Cruz walk by and I thought, *Screw you*, as I sat at my desk. *I could do a much better job than you.* But inside, I panicked. I paced the floor in my office. I couldn't think of anything to get back at him. I started obsessing. I had to come up with a plan quickly. Then it came to me, so I went back to a tried and true method.

I waited until finally, everyone left and Mr. Cruz was alone. I hid behind a cabinet, slipped off my bra and panties, and headed back to my desk, desperately thinking about how to best to approach him. There was no way I was going back under the bridge. At last, I walked into his office and sat on one of the chairs farther back from his desk, without crossing my legs. "Is there anything else I can do before I leave for the day?" I asked.

Clearly Mr. Cruz was shaken when he looked up and caught a glimpse.

"No, no, Ms. Preston," he said abruptly. "That will be all; have a good evening."

I felt like a wild animal in a cage unable to get the prey in front of me. I thought I had missed my chance to get him. I had to be more patient; after all, he hadn't actually rejected me.

I stayed up much of the night thinking of how to get Mr. Cruz. Finally, it hit me at 3:30 am. I decided to prepare a letter to the board as if I was a witness to Mr. Cruz abusing his employee, in this case me. It was a masterpiece. I was proud, and if it were in other circumstances, I knew Mr. Cruz would have been impressed. I sent it out anonymously the next morning on the way to work. It read something like this:

Dear Members:

I have witnessed Mr. Cruz treat Ms. Preston in a sexual and demeaning manner at the office, and I think the board should intervene on her behalf.

Signed,

Anonymous

Despite my bloodshot eyes the next day, I was satisfied that I would get Mr. Cruz for what he said to me.

Outside my window, I noticed Charles walking to wherever he goes in the early mornings and late afternoons. This time I followed him to an area outside the building reserved for smokers. As I rounded the corner, I could hear him laughing and joking with Simon Daniels, Mr. Cruz's boss. I rubbed my eyes, and walked up to Charles, feigning some of my best tears.

"What's wrong, Amanda?" he asked.

It was a chance to turn up the flames on Cruz, I thought to myself.

"Mr. Cruz tried to touch me in his office last night, Charles," I choked in a whispering voice loud enough for those nearby to hear.

Mr. Daniels, feeling uncomfortable about the situation, immediately put out his cigarette and walked away.

Charles stayed with me until my bout of crying had passed.

"You'll be fine, Amanda," he said.

I hugged Charles as he continued to comfort me.

Mr. Cruz has no idea who he is dealing with, I told myself with a smile and sigh of deep satisfaction.

When I returned to the office Monday morning, Clark, the company attorney, was sitting at my desk with a smirk on his face. A six-foot man so grossly overweight you could hear his inner thighs rubbing across the hallway. Everyone avoided him like the plague because of his lack of personal hygiene that could permeate clothing and even walls it seemed. His reputation for being a bully and a coward certainly didn't help him win any friends either. It probably had something to do with the obvious chip on his shoulder. He was a hard ass. *Someone like him should come with a warning label*, I thought. Still, I needed him if I had any chance of taking Cruz's job. Playing it cool was what I was all about, and now it was my turn to charm the fat man. I was about to learn what he wanted from me.

"Good morning, Amanda," he said. *Even his voice sounds*

fat, I thought to myself.

"I heard about Cruz. What he did to you was wrong, and he's paying for it. I'm seeing to it," he said.

"I appreciate all you've done for me," I said with a hint of tears and a sniff.

"I don't know what's happening to the men around here; they seem to think they can do as they please," Clark said, as his eyes drifted down to see if I was wearing a bra. "You don't have to worry about Mr. Cruz anymore, Amanda. He is done, gone. We had an emergency meeting late last night. He resigned; said he is finished. Actually saw him cry; his wife and members of the board cried too. I couldn't believe it. I heard he took it especially hard because one day he would have to explain to his four daughters that he was accused of sexually harassing a woman. He's a broken man," he declared with a chubby smirk.

"Guess all them poor homeless people he was gunna save will just have to keep living under the bridges," he said, laughing.

Screw em, that's where they belong, I said to myself. *Maybe that man will stab them all and they will shut the hell up.*

"It's a sad thing, Clark," I said aloud wiping my eye to show concern.

His eyes followed me the entire time while I walked over to open the window. *What a piece of shit*, I thought to myself, Clark had nothing on Cruz. Clark was like most men, no challenge, no brains, a less evolved species. I turned back to look at Clark, it was too easy. "You're going to recommend me for the job," I stated.

He didn't even flinch.

"What do I get out of the deal Amanda?" he quickly responded.

A pathetic excuse for a human and more of a pervert, I was sure there was something he would want from me later down the road.

"Whatever you want," I replied confidently while bending down to pick up a pen.

"Good, I'm glad we understand each other," he said as he stood up. "If you can get Charles on board, it's a done deal." As usual, Clark walked out leaving his stench behind.

CHAPTER 22

TAKING OUT THE OFFICE GARBAGE

CHARLES WASN'T REALLY MY TYPE. ACTUALLY, I DIDN'T KNOW if I had a type. Nonetheless, he had influence with Daniels. My co-workers eagerly spilled everything I needed to know about Charles. There were only two important things to me: his love of the outdoors and his multiple affairs, about which his long-term girlfriend was oblivious. How pathetic, I thought to myself.

I stood at my desk and caught a glimpse of Charles coming in late as usual. Charles is what I came to call muddy. Thirty-something, and close to five feet ten with blackish red hair and a light reddish beard. If not for being well-placed in a middle management position, he no doubt would have been working at the local donut hole. Put there by the hand of someone else, he was lazy, not expected to work, content to ride on the coattails of others. Charles was a male whore with implied permission from management to screw any girl in the company he could get his hands on. Charles was all about casual sex. I had learned a long time ago, one person always gets more out of a screw than the other, and tonight that person would be me.

The afternoon cigarette break area was alive and well with chatter about Mr. Cruz leaving the company, until I showed up. Charles gestured for me to sit next to him.

"How are you feeling, Amanda? Maybe you need some comforting," he said.

Still trying to get into my pants, Charles never let up.

"I'm feeling sad for Mr. Cruz," I said. "He was a mentor to me." Then I said under my breath, "Meet me for a drink at *The 66* today after work. Tomorrow is Saturday anyway, and I need to talk to someone. You're the only one who has really been there for me, Charles."

Charles's eyes opened wide. "I'll be there," he said.

A few cocktails in, I opened up to Charles about how Mr. Cruz had propositioned and tried to touch me. I described every detail of how I rejected his advances and threatened to tell his wife. Charles said he heard the company would be making me a money offer in the next few weeks to drop the complaint. "It's not the money, Charles," I said crying, "I'm still in shock."

Hoping to console and distract me from the situation with Mr. Cruz, Charles offered to escort me to a nearby "inn".

Walking through the parking lot slightly intoxicated, I turned and kissed Charles on the mouth. We stayed lip-to-lip for a few steps and stumbled into the front office desk. Charles didn't have any money, so I took out my credit card. The woman at the front desk looked at me, surprised that I would be paying. "Mind your own damn business," I yelled pointing my finger at her face. It had already been five months since that piece of shit Drake raped me; I had come back as strong as ever and was ready to use sex again to my advantage. I could care less what a two-bit front desk clerk thought. I figured a short letter to her boss about her attitude might be appropriate after I was finished with Charles.

We continued feeling each other all the way to the room. While holding the door for Charles, my senses picked up his strong pungent perspiration. He reeked of saturated smoke from cigarettes and a bad diet. I tried to hold my breath a couple of times while he was kissing my neck.

His cold hands went up my blouse and quickly found my breasts. He had already unzipped his pants and started stroking his penis. He kept taking shots from a bottle of tequila he'd gotten from his car, at one time pouring a few drops on himself.

"Lick it off, Amanda," he said.

"What?" I asked.

"Lick it off," he repeated.

I sat on the chair licking him as he lay on the bed. It felt strange, familiar.

Over and over I began to use my mouth to help him get hard. *This is so similar to my dream*, I thought, pausing for a second. My eyes focused toward the closet. Before I let myself think more of my dream, I took a mouthful of tequila and guzzled it down.

He lit up a cigarette. "I just need a moment," he said.

Enticing as I could be, I stood at the edge of the bed and removed my blouse, letting my breasts slowly drop out from my bra. I turned to reveal my thong, watching him harden from the show. It was a turn-on for me too, as he lay naked on the bedspread, touching himself. He managed to slide on the condom. As I moved closer, he sat up to kiss my breasts. His smokey breath made me slightly nauseous as I moved to straddle him. Charles entered me quickly and pulled me downward to feel his entire shaft, as if to revel in his manhood. There was a foul odor emanating from the mixture of our bodies as he continued thrusting in and out.

He held me upward and pulled me hard onto him over and over again. I felt myself coming to a hard climax, screaming as he let out a grunt. My own fluids quickly began leaking down between my thighs.

I awoke the next morning feeling subdued. Quietly, I crawled sideways out of the messy bed. My panties lay on the dirty carpet stained with red wine or blood, I wasn't sure. *Maybe something leftover from Officer Drake*, I thought to myself, so I stuck them in my purse. Lightly lifting up the blanket, I found my blue bra. Charles's underwear lay in full view at the edge of the bed. They appeared yellowish and dingy. I couldn't help but feel a small amount of throw-up in my mouth as I pulled the strap of my bra out. I would have left it, but it cost me ninety dollars and I didn't want to buy another one. Charles lay still in bed not making a sound.

Typical of a one-night stand, he knew the drill: the next morning communication was prohibited. He respectfully waited for me to leave.

After snapping the clip on my bra, I quickly pulled my dress over my head. My eyes momentarily fixed on a tiny creature crawling along the wall on the bathroom floor. Surprised, I dared not make a sound that might cause Charles to move or speak.

Walking lightly to the door, I looked at the tawdry décor of the hotel room: animal-print bedspread, mirrors on the wall, ceiling with remnants of past repairs, and a pungent smell of old. The half-empty bottle of cheap tequila sat on the small table near the bed.

My part was done. Charles was a person in power and now I would have its advantages. *Quid pro quo*, I said to myself walking down the stairs. I shook my head a little—as if to clean and clear - and rolled my eyes; this game was getting a bit old and tiring, and far too easy anymore.

CHAPTER 23

THE CONGRESSMAN

FOR THE SECOND NIGHT IN A ROW, I WAS AWAKENED BY the constant singing of a blackbird on a street light outside my bedroom window. When I opened my eyes I saw the reflection of a green light blinking on my phone. Clark had sent me a text message. I was in! He managed to get a last minute vote by proxy from the members of the board to place me as temporary CEO of Madison.

"You're in charge, Amanda. It's time to shake things up a bit," it said. "I'll be by your new office at eight a.m."

Things were moving fast, and though it was still dark outside, I decided to get to Madison early. Luckily, I already had the gold-plated plaque in my purse with my name for the door. As I began my victory strut along Park Avenue, I couldn't help but join the blackbird in song; "Screw you, screw you Cruz," I sang over and over. "I am a God." It was a favorite place of mine to walk, and it felt even sweeter to savor my victory like this.

I arrived at Madison before anyone could see me. One or two lowly staffers were there already, so I walked quickly, wanting no one to disturb me in my new office. When I opened the door, I was greeted by the smell of old leather and stale ink. Though it permeated the walls and furnishings, it was perfect for me. I felt completely at ease and in control. I sat and leaned back in the padded burgundy high-backed chair and surveyed my new kingdom.

The office came with a spectacular view of the city. As the few pre-dawn lights competed with the rising sun, I gazed out at the adjacent high-rise office buildings. I stood and looked out the window, down to a reflecting pond below where I could see white puffy clouds amid the changing pastels of the morning sky.

How easy it is for people to believe what is reflected on the outside, I thought. *Never knowing what is hidden beneath in the depths. They can't see the real me, but I can sense every part of them. Here I am in this big office heading a major public financial corporation. Huh, I don't even balance my own checking account. No matter. I am in the game—shit, I'm a major player in the game—and I did it without having to expose any real part of me. This is where I have always belonged. At the top, in control, making all the decisions.*

On a nearby table sat a box with a photograph of Cruz with his wife and daughters sitting on a park swing. I heard the rumblings of more people outside the office and quickly placed the picture in my purse, thinking it might come in useful someday. I walked to shut the door, but before it closed, my nose was met with a familiar stench. My loyal lackey Clark was nearby.

"Have you read the morning paper, Amanda?" Clark asked breathlessly, bursting in.

Of course, I read it, and you smell like shit, I thought to myself.

"No, I haven't, Clark. Good morning to you. Why, is there something about Madison?" I asked.

"It's an article about Cruz. He is so humiliated, you really burned him. You take no prisoners," he said with a laugh.

Standing at the door was a black-haired medium-build intelligent-looking young woman.

"I'm Sylvia, Ms. Preston, your administrative secretary. I'm sorry to have to bring this up right away, but there is an important matter that needs immediate attention. Members of the Board are here, including Congressman Easton. They called an emergency meeting early this morning. Should I have them wait in the boardroom, Ms. Preston?" she asked.

"Yes," Clark quickly jumped in. "Let them know we will be there in fifteen minutes."

"What do we do Clark?" I asked after she left. I was a bit ruffled at the surprise news, but didn't let it show. I quickly put on my tough game face. "What the hell do they want?"

"They don't really know you Amanda. Remember that it was a proxy vote that put you here. They want a meet-and-greet to be sure you can handle the job. There's nothing to worry about. I'll brief you on all our investments, here and abroad. All you have to do is show them you're familiar with it all and they will leave us alone."

"What about this Congressman Easton? Why is he here?"

"Relax. Same thing. He happens to be the largest stock-holder, with thirty-six percent. Just be confident and charming like you know how to be and we'll get through this." His eyes looked up and away for a second, and then he smiled. "Cruz brought in new money just before he left; I'll tell the board it was you who secured the investments. It's a cool thirty million." He chuckled at his own stroke of genius with that idea.

And I had to hand it to him. With that help, my meeting with the board went remarkably well. Of course, the members were all men, so my charm was well received to say the least. By lunchtime I had been unanimously voted CEO of Madison Financial and awarded an impressive seven figure salary.

After a long lunch, I learned more about each of the members, but I was focused on Congressman Easton; there was something about him that intrigued me. I could sense the power of his office from his very presence. I complimented his every move until he became interested in me. It turned out he was a senior member of the Arms Services Committee and had direct access to the President. This was a whole new power that I needed to add to my repertoire. *Maybe I can meet the President,* I thought to myself, *and offer my services.* Now I had an in to Washington politics.

Congressman Easton was tall, well-mannered and attractive for a man in his late sixties. He kind of reminded me of Bob. His gray hair and custom-made suits gave me the impression he was probably open to "lobby" money which everybody knows was just another word for taking a bribe. But I knew he was intimately tied to Madison. His stake was really just another way of saying we had his money. And that could become my power.

Clark and I went over the Congressman's portfolio the very next day. Over the past ten years he had been socking away large sums of money at Madison, not only under his own name, but for members of his family. I found that many of the deposits came from an offshore account, one that traced back to a weapons dealer in another country. It was a front for a fake corporation set up to pay the Congressman to promote military action in obscure places around the world. The longer he continued to send business to this friend of his, the more money it meant for Madison, and for my quarterly bonus. This was also my edge to tap into some real power.

Obviously, charming the Congressman was not a big challenge. He was still in town, and we met later that evening for cocktails. He warmed up quickly, and confided in me about some of his fetishes. *Another sick bastard.* I didn't care. I decided I would drug him if need be, like someone did to Scully those many years ago. I didn't need to have sex anymore to get what I wanted.

"With you at the helm of Madison, we could do great things together, Amanda," he said, hoping I would accommodate his perversions. *Sure*, I thought, as I smiled at him.

The next month I was his guest in Washington D.C. I was picked up in a government vehicle, and the Congressman had the driver take me to a downtown restaurant that I knew was well known for discussions of high dollar politics. I was pleasantly surprised to see the Congressman standing outside talking with the Chairman of the Federal Treasury and Banking Committee whom I had just seen on the morning news. I smiled to myself, *this was a whole new ballgame of politics, money and power.*

"Good afternoon Amanda. Welcome to D.C. From the moment I met you, I knew I wanted to get to know you more," he said. "I have a feeling we are of the same ilk. I think you'll like it here."

After a few drinks, Congressman Easton started spilling his government secrets. "Can I trust you?" he asked, leaning right up to my face with slurred speech.

"Of course Congressman. You can trust me," I answered. "What can I do for you?"

"This morning in session, we decided to bomb a dictator. The worst type; torture, rape, mass killings, it's atrocious. We have enough intelligence and unilateral approval to support a military strike by local rebels, and most likely permanently remove him. If we don't, we project eight to ten thousand civilian deaths in the next few months. The problem is that I have this ... friend ... who won't be ready with the weapons for another month or two, and I really like to buy from him. He takes care of me and I do the same for him." He paused slightly and looked straight at me. "Do you think it's wrong for me to wait Amanda?" he asked.

Let me see if I got this straight, I thought. The Congressman is asking me if he should wait and let people die so he can make a lot of money? He doesn't know them; I don't know them either, and I just put an offer on a new upscale condo. What do I care if they die? What do I care about someone else's cause? The country is probably over-populated anyway. I need to convince him to wait so he can get that kickback from his friend into his offshore account. He doesn't know that I've put all this together, but hell if I am going to let some poor people half way around the world take profits away from me. I deserve my own place and nice furnishings worthy of my status. All he wants is reassurance in this case; he doesn't even want sex.

"Congressman, I'm sure your friend provides the best weapons that would help the rebels really get the job done right, wouldn't you say? Without that, if you were to rush, even more might die in the end." I gave him my best calm, reassuring voice and smile, knowing that's all I needed to push him. "Besides, taking care of the people you know is always the right thing to do."

"You're a breath of fresh air Amanda. I really appreciate your thoughts on this," he cheerfully replied. "Let's stop talking shop and celebrate our friendship."

Sure enough, two months later, Madison received a hefty deposit from an offshore account, in the name of Manny Easton, whoever that was. After several million more from another primary investor (this game was so easy), our company's stock rose and split. Clark kept the underlings on task maximizing profits, and I was able to pocket another seven figures in bonuses. I paid for my condo in cash and now I'm looking to buy a little something on Capitol Hill as well.

My success at Madison became well publicized in several international financial journals. Congressman Easton has even been quoted on how much he values my opinion and that he calls on me often for advice. It's certainly been a good relationship for me. I've gotten to know the ins and outs and the key players out there. There is so much potential for me.

Sometimes these days, when I'm in the bath enjoying a glass of champagne, I think about the people in that far off land, their pitiful lives, if they still have lives.

CHAPTER 24

FINAL MEETING

SINCE THINGS WERE GOING SO WELL FOR ME AT MADISON and with the Congressman I decided it was time for me to take a much deserved stroll at my favorite place on Park Avenue. As I was nearing the fountain, I noticed a man in his mid-sixties walking toward me in the opposite direction. Something tingled deep down inside of me right away. *What was it about him?* Then I realized that his resemblance to the man in the glass on the subway those years ago in New York was kind of eerie. He seemed to notice me as we passed, but he was wearing sunglasses and I couldn't be sure. I felt drawn to him. When I looked back, he was stopped; he had turned around and was standing looking directly at me. His thick salt and pepper wavy hair gleamed in the sun.

Unable to think, I turned also and began walking towards him.

He kept his sunglasses on as I got closer.

"Hi…Do I know you?" he asked.

"It's me Amanda, Daddy. Were you on the subway in New York? Have you been following me?" I asked.

"No, this is the first time I've seen you, since you left. You look wonderful, Amanda," he said. I almost felt him looking me up and down.

Daddy looked handsome. I was reminded that I too share his charm and debonair style.

"It really is you." I said excitedly. "You looked familiar when we passed and I noticed your black shiny hair. Where's Mother?"

"Your Mother is dead, Amanda. She took some pills and never woke up, kind of like what happened to Scully. She's been gone for several years."

"What about Jamie, Daddy? Where is he?"

"He went to college, got married, and now he lives in Washington, D.C. I haven't heard from him for a long time."

"What are you doing here, Daddy?" I asked. "Are you here for work?"

"No, Amanda, I came for you." As he turned, Daddy removed his sunglasses revealing the most beautiful blue eyes I had ever seen. So blue, they pierced me. It was like an instantaneous shock to my brain.

I immediately flashed to when I was a little girl standing next to him. I was holding a roll of clear wrapping watching Daddy move two large things.

"What are you putting in my closet Daddy?" I asked.

"I want you to save these for me Amanda. It will be our secret," he said.

My mind flashed back to Daddy's face.

I suddenly felt weak. *How could this be?* I asked myself. *This can't be true. Not Daddy.......*

Slowly, I turned away in the other direction.

"How about getting together this evening for dinner Amanda?" he asked.

"Yes, Daddy," I said pausing to answer. "That's a good idea. How about something at Mateo's at around six? That'll give us a couple of hours to freshen up," I said.

"I'll meet you there, Amanda," he said.

When Daddy turned to walk away, I somehow knew he had been stalking me. I sensed it. I quickly crossed over to the stoplight and began thinking of my childhood. *I never saw him because of his traveling. I really didn't know him. His eyes, how could I not remember? And what about Mother? She was gone. That's why she never picked up the phone when I called. Maybe she died right after she took me to college. Did he kill her? Is Jamie really in D.C, or did Daddy do something to him? Did Daddy come here to kill me? Was it his face in the subway?*

Several thoughts continued processing in my mind as I hurried to my loft.

With each passing moment, it seemed as if a door in my mind was opening, revealing more details of when I was a little girl growing up. I pictured Daddy and Mother sitting on the living room couch watching television, but they were always looking away from me. I couldn't remember seeing their faces, ever. But, Mother was always watching over me day and night and wouldn't leave me alone. *Was she actually protecting me, not hovering and hating me?*

I began to think of Kevin, the little boy that went missing from my school. He came to my dreams and tried to tell me something. I remembered telling Daddy about him just before he went missing. There was a lady in my dreams too, that looked as though she was being hurt. *Did Daddy have something to do with hurting them? Is my brain connected to Daddy's in some way, like Dr. Samson said?*

When I got closer to my door, it was wide open. The place had been ransacked. The manager came up and told me he had seen an intruder and called the police. When I went inside, nothing appeared to have been taken except for a diary I kept of some of my doctor's sessions. It was clear to me now that Daddy saw me as a threat. He knew that I could expose him. He came for me, just like he said. I was his target.

The police arrived and I provided a statement of the only item missing. There was no need to meet Daddy at Mateo's anymore. He made his presence known. The encounter and the break-in left me nervous. I stayed awake all night standing by the edge of my window behind the curtain looking into the street, knowing Daddy was out there, both outside my apartment and inside my mind.

On my way home from the office, I continued to wait around the fountain where Daddy and I met, carefully looking to see if he was there. I couldn't see him, but I knew he was watching me. For the next few days I sat on the fountain edge by the water thinking of my life as a child, and of Mother. So many questions still flooded my mind. Each day when I arrived home, I turned off the lights and peeked through the curtain to be sure he couldn't see me, but I knew it was a matter of time before we would meet again.

I remembered more details like when I pictured Sarah's mom Mari hugging Mother. *Why was Mother crying?*

On the third night, exhausted, I lay on the bed, finally closing my eyes to sleep.

My dream quickly took me to the closet doors of my old room to perform my usual routine. I took out the man's body and sat it on the couch and then I placed the woman's body on the counter a few feet away. The desire to open them was particularly strong this time. The woman seemed different. She was trying especially hard to move, but the wrap was too tight. She was insistent. But, the urge of the man seemed to be just as strong. I could feel his power trying to stop me from going to the woman. *He is in my consciousness*, I thought to myself.

Then like before, the woman's finger began slowly moving. It was pushing up over and over stretching the plastic. I stared at it, when it suddenly jabbed through the wrapping. Horror came over me as a familiar gold ring with three diamonds showed itself. I lay petrified from the vision of my mother's wedding ring on the woman's finger. Still in a dream state, "Mother! Mother," I screamed. I woke, in a cold sweat.

The morning alarm abruptly struck its high note and I jumped up with a jolt. I rushed to the bathroom to wipe the sweat from my forehead and splashed cold water over and over onto my face. The visions of Mother and faces of people I had never met, swam before my eyes like a wall of photographs in front of me. I collapsed onto the bathroom floor, struggling to breathe like the man by the river. I wailed with a sound as if mother herself was in the room with me.

I began to fall into a dreary sense of helplessness, of emptiness and gloom. I closed my eyes. The comfort from a sudden light breeze brushed the side of my face. The warm feel of her cheek on mine was soft and tender as I pictured Mother's face smiling down at me, "I love you, Amanda," she said. I placed my hand in Mother's and squeezed it, as if to let her know it was okay. "I love you mother," I said. I felt such relief, like a huge weight had been lifted for maybe the first time in my life.

When I sat up, the mirror on the door showed my face with beautiful sparkled tears just like Sarah's. I breathed a sigh and placed my hand on my heart to hold its brokenness. Mother never left me. She had always tried to help me. She knew it wasn't my fault what I had become; she knew I was a reflection of Daddy.

The next day I was still dazed from the experience and the newly found emotion. I left work early and walked straight to the fountain where I found Daddy. He was dressed to the nines, charming a beautiful woman he had just met. When he saw me, he began to walk away.

"Daddy, don't leave so soon," I said quickly. "We really should have that dinner I promised. I'm sorry I couldn't make it last time. You know, things come up."

"Yes, Amanda, it's time we got together, isn't it?" he asked with a grin.

"Come over tonight Daddy, to my loft around seven. You know where it is right?" I said with a smile. "Besides, I can make your favorite dish, linguini vongole, it's your favorite if I remember correctly."

"That's an invitation that's hard to turn down my dear," he said, "I'll see you tonight Amanda." As daddy was walking away, he turned back to look at me long enough to give me his most charming smile.

He didn't bother to ask for my address. There was no need. We both knew he had been there before. That's how it works for people like us. No real feelings, just an act. I figured he would try to make it quick and deadly. I wouldn't see it coming, just like he did with Mother.

But I knew I could still have power over him. As I recalled, he couldn't resist the thought of touching my beautiful body, especially when I was a little girl.

Tonight, I will give him the thing he desires most of all.

Seven came quickly. Daddy was punctual, as always.

I was a little surprised that he didn't seem suspicious of me at all. In the end, even he, was like all other men, easily distracted and anxious to confirm their egos and manhood.

Yes, I did answer the door wearing only my stilettos, so obviously he must have figured out that I remembered all the abuse from childhood. But he probably thought I actually liked it, that he was that good.

He drained his glass of champagne with excitement and vigor. I was anxious and quickly poured him another so we could appropriately toast our reunion. I have to admit though, I was a little disappointed in Daddy; he was not the connoisseur I thought he was, certainly not as much as I had become. He wasn't able to recognize the aftertaste of Scully's medicine mixed into his glass of La Grand Dame, I figured it was perfect for the occasion).

Even now, it's hard to forget his expression when he realized he was helpless; he just sat there staring motionless at the table while I finished dinner. I made it clear we had to eat before any carnal pleasures, but that also gave me the chance to catch him up on school, New York, my marriage to Bob, Officer Drake and the many other experiences in my life so far. I must have bored him after an hour with all the details because he finally closed his eyes.

When I was finished eating, I laid him down on the floor so he would be more comfortable. I thanked him for the perfect evening and for being a gentleman. He pleasantly surprised me. I didn't expect his eyes to open again and when I started wrapping him in plastic, he got so excited, it just made everything so much better.

I'm not sure how long it took him to finally, really die

because his eyes were still fluttering when I put him in the closet. I haven't checked, but I figured I would leave him in there until I had time to dispose of the body.

I went back to the living room to finish the dessert and champagne.

EPILOGUE

UNABLE TO GET HER OUT OF MY HEAD, I BECAME CONCERNED for her well-being, I found several addresses among the many notes I had taken to write her life story. The first took me to a dilapidated apartment complex, with a dark hallway littered with trash and a stairwell with broken handrails. The manager was unable to provide any information from the photograph I had of her and suggested it could be her but with a different shade of hair color. No record of her existed. The second address was a number and street name I found on a separate yellow sheet of paper she used to doodle on during our sessions. After an hour drive to the city, I found myself parked outside an upscale high-rise apartment in Nob Hill.

The entrance of the building was tall and wide. A doorman stood in front of the large brass doors blocking the public from seeing the residents coming and going. I waited until I caught a glimpse of a glamorous woman with a tall, handsome man on her arm. The long auburn hair could not conceal the pale skin, piercing blue eyes and long, flowing red gown I had seen before, nor the lavish jewels with which she was bedecked. I watched as she stepped into a waiting black limousine.

I remembered something she once told me: "As long as

there are men, someone like me will always have an opening to come in and do as she likes. Their vulnerability to women causes them to turn against their friends and family with the simple hope of sex. It is they who have created people like me. How pathetic is that," she said.

The answer to my question became obvious that Saturday afternoon. It was clear: Amanda had chosen me either consciously or subconsciously because she had a story she thought could make a difference, and though I became fond of her, Amanda was finished with me and had gone off to live her life, or so I thought...

Not a day goes by that I don't think who out there is not aware they are in the crosshairs of a sociopath.

LETTERS FROM A SOCIOPATH

Dear Mr. Barnes,

Mr. Dean from your Legal Division has been pressuring me to date him, and I think he should be terminated. He does not respect sexual harassment or no fraternizing policies. I refuse to sign this letter for fear of reprisals, but I will go to the press if nothing is done.

Anonymous

To Members of the Board

I am an employee working here and I would like to report that I have witnessed management harassing Ms. Amanda Preston. I think someone should look into it quickly before it gets out of hand.

Jennifer Cranston
Delwood Lane
Greenwich, Connecticut

Hi Jennifer,

Just a little note to let you know that I had a great time with your husband in Europe. We had so much fun, in so many different ways, and positions. Don't bother trying to find out who this is (although I will tell you that we work together). Oh, and good luck with your marriage.

Moore Pool Services
89 Carroll St.
Sunnyvale, Calif.

Dear Mr. Moore,

Your pool boy stayed sleeping by my pool most of the day and drinking alcohol. I watched him the entire morning and would like you to look into this matter. If you must send him back, be sure he works the full day. I will not be paying you for the day he slept.

Regards,

Amanda Preston

Dalton Labor Services

N. 1st. St.. San Jose

Dear Mr. Towers.

I believe the worker you sent over to do our landscaping has been looking through my personal belongings. I found several of my undergarments out of order and they appear as though someone is purposely moving them from one drawer to another. Please see to it that your worker is properly dealt with or I will not be recommending your services to any of our friends. and I will report the matter to the authorities.

Regards.

Amanda Preston

Tom's Dry Cleaners

Hillsdale Blvd.

San Mateo. Calif.

Dear Mr. Sams.

On November 26 I picked up my dry cleaning from your store and your clerk. the one with the black mustache and dark skin. stared at me in a way that I felt threatened.

I was very uncomfortable with his posture and don't believe

having someone like that working there is a good idea. Please terminate him immediately.

Regards,

Amanda Preston

Expert Auto Garage
Monroe St.
Santa Clara. Calif.

I was at your facility last month and I saw the man behind the register putting twenty dollar bills in his pocket. I believe he was stealing and should be arrested. Please look into this for me.

Regards,

Amanda Preston

LETTERS FROM A SOCIOPATH

Police Report Filed

Complainant: Amanda Preston

Assigned to Officer Adams

Gas being stolen from her parked vehicle at her residence. Nothing showing on security cameras. She thinks it is her neighbor. Officers at scene found no evidence, confirmed tank was full.

Police Report Filed

Complainant: Amanda Preston

Assigned to Officer Jennings

Please look into this matter. Ms. Preston from 8775 Sanders has reported that her landlord has been breaking into her apartment and looking over her financial statements. According to Ms. Preston, the landlord has a way of not being detected by security cameras.

Senate Committee on Appropriations

Dear Mr. Chairman,

It has come to my attention that certain members of your Committee have been engaging in inappropriate activities. I certainly would not want these activities to come to light to make you look unfavorable. I was wondering if we might have a chance to meet and discuss the situation.

Your loyal constituent,

Ms. Amanda Preston

CPSIA information can be obtained at www.ICGtesting.com
Printed in the USA
BVOW05s0615080914

365804BV00001B/35/P

9 780988 261600